CAROLINE LAWRENCE

THE

ROMAN
MYSTERIES
TREASURY

Orion
Children's Books

First published in Great Britain in 2007
by Orion Children's Books
a division of the Orion Publishing Group Ltd
Orion House
5 Upper St Martin's Lane
London WC2H 9EA
An Hachette Livre UK Company

1 3 5 7 9 10 8 6 4 2

The Orion Publishing Group's policy is to use papers
that are natural, renewable and recyclable products and
made from wood grown in sustainable forests. The
logging and manufacturing processes are expected to
conform to the environmental regulations of the
country of origin.

A catalogue record for this book is available from the
British Library

Printed in Italy by Rotolito Lombarda SpA

ISBN 978 1 84255 602 3

www.orionbooks.co.uk
www.romanmysteries.com

Book designed by Dave Crook

CONTENTS

To Pekka Tuomisto,
Latin scholar par excellence,
who proofreads the Roman Mysteries
and translates them into Finnish,
and who came up with the word 'detectrix'

INTRODUCTION

OSTIA, THE KALENDS OF MARCH AD 80

SALVE! My name is Flavia Gemina, daughter of Marcus Flavius Geminus, sea captain. I love solving mysteries. It's my favourite thing to do in the world. Why? Because I hate injustice. (And I hate not knowing things!)

I call myself a 'detectrix', which means a female person who uncovers the truth. Some people in Ostia disapprove of me. They say a proper Roman girl of the equestrian class should stay inside and spin wool and not run about claiming to solve mysteries. But what is more important? Wool? Or the Truth? Besides, lots of other people are glad I solve mysteries. Especially those whose children I recently helped rescue from kidnappers.

As well as solving mysteries, I love reading and writing. Therefore, as today is traditionally the first day of the new year – the Kalends of March – I have decided to write my first book.

I met the great scholar Admiral Pliny last August, and I was with him when he

tragically died in the terrible eruption of Vesuvius. He once told me that he hoped his books will be read thousands of years from now, and that if they were, it would be a kind of immortality. Everyone dies, he said, but if people read your words and discover your thoughts, then it's as if you're still alive.

I have a copy of his *Natural History*

(all thirty-seven scrolls!) and it's true. Whenever I read his words it's as if he's sitting right here beside me, chatting to me and giving me advice.

So that is what I am going to do in this book. I am going to record my life so far as if I were writing for people living thousands of years in the future. And because I don't know everything (yet!) I have asked some of my friends and family to contribute, too.

I have given them each assignments, like my tutor Aristo gives me work, and asked them to write short essays. I also asked each of them to write a short biography about themselves.

Oh, and I am going to intersperse the essays with quotes from some of my favourite authors (Aristo says he will help me with this) and with other lists compiled by my friends and family.

I hope that as you read this book you will feel that we are sitting right there beside you.

Some of the words in this book may look strange. If you don't know them, 'Aristo's Scroll' on pages 114-118 will tell you what they mean and how to pronounce them.

FLAVIA GEMINA

FULL NAME: Flavia Marci filia Gemina of the Voturia tribe

BIRTHDAY: 16 June AD 69

ELEMENT: Air

BIRTHPLACE: Ostia, the port of Rome

EYE COLOUR: Blue-grey

HAIR COLOUR: Light brown (flavus means 'tawny')

FAVOURITE FOOD: Cold roast chicken and salad with garum dressing

FAVOURITE PLACE: Sitting on the marble bench in my garden, with a scroll

FAVOURITE TIME OF DAY: Dusk on a summer's evening

MY TOPICS: A Day in My Life, Festivals and Holidays, Myths and Legends

I live in the town of Ostia, which is the port of Rome. My house is on Green Fountain Street and it is built right into the town wall. In fact my bedroom window looks out onto the necropolis, the city of the dead. The graveyard makes me feel both sad and happy. The ashes of my mother Myrtilla are in a tomb out there. She died in childbirth when I was only three years old. My twin baby brothers died, too. Their ashes are in two little urns next to hers.

But looking out at the necropolis also makes me feel happy because that was where I solved my first mystery. The mystery was who stole my father's signet ring. I found the culprit and it was then that I realised my life's calling: to be a detectrix, a truth-seeker.

My father – Marcus Flavius Geminus, sea captain – is the head of the household, the paterfamilias. I love him very much, but he can be quite strict and so I don't mind when he's away on one of his voyages. When he's gone, I am the 'daughterfamilias' and can do almost anything I like! I can tell the other members of the household what to do:

my friend Nubia, my old nursemaid Alma, our door slave Caudex and our two dogs. Not so much Aristo, though. He is my very nice tutor: young and handsome with curly hair and long eyelashes. He comes from Corinth in Greece and sometimes he helps me and my friends solve mysteries. I can't really boss Aristo around like the others, but if I'm crafty I can make him tell me to do something I already want to do. Like solve mysteries.

A DAY IN MY LIFE

Here is an average day for me.

My dog Scuto wakes me at sunrise. He presses his cold nose into my face and I open my eyes to see his face looming in a big, panting grin. If I've been up late the night before, I roll over and go back to sleep. Scuto knows it's no good trying to wake me if I'm tired, so he goes downstairs to help our cook Alma prepare breakfast. She has already been out to buy bread and is usually back by dawn.

Soon I hear the beautiful sound of flute and lyre. Nubia usually plays music with Aristo first thing in the morning. Nubia used to be my slave-girl but she saved my life so many times that finally I set her free. Now she's like my dark-skinned sister. If Scuto doesn't get me up, the music does.

Nubia likes clothes and jewellery but I'm not really bothered about such things. I lace up my sandals and slip on any old tunic, a short one in summer and a long one in winter. Then I go downstairs. Our house has a secret garden inside: nobody on the street can see it. In the centre is a fountain. I splash some water on my face and have a drink. Then I use the latrine. This month it's my job to empty the latrine bucket every morning – but that's another story.

We all eat breakfast whenever we come downstairs: usually a warm poppy-seed roll and a piece of cheese in summer and a hot poculum made of spiced wine mixed with milk in winter.

By the time I appear, pater is usually at work in his study, preparing for the day ahead. He calls the whole household together into the atrium and we watch him make the daily offering at the lararium, the household shrine. It might be a honey-cake, or a piece of fruit, or a hyacinth-scented candle. Just something to keep the household gods happy.

After morning prayers, pater goes out to call on his patron Cordius. Then he visits the barber and goes to wait at his office in the Forum of the Corporations for his own clients to call. They are mainly sailors and other people whom he might employ on his voyages. He's out a lot at the moment because the sailing season is about to begin.

After pater leaves, at about an hour past dawn, Jonathan and Lupus come over for lessons. Jonathan is my next-door-neighbour. He's Jewish. We became friends after he saved me from some wild dogs. I like Jonathan because he makes me laugh. Lupus is a boy we discovered running wild in the necropolis outside the town walls. He can't speak. He's a bit wild but very clever. He learned to read in less than a month and now he can write, too. Lupus lives with Jonathan.

The boys have lessons with Nubia and me. Jonathan's father Mordecai is a doctor. He and my father came to some arrangement. I think Doctor Mordecai gives us free medical care in return for

Aristo's tutoring. Jonathan's older sister Miriam attended lessons with us once or twice, but now she's married and has moved away. She's fifteen and the most beautiful girl I have ever seen.

Aristo teaches us Latin literature, Greek language, mythology, philosophy and maths. (I hate maths almost as much as I hate emptying the latrine bucket.)

Lessons last until noon, when the gongs announce the opening of the public baths. Then we have a light lunch of bread and cheese and olives. Afterwards the adults take a siesta or go to the baths. That's when we solve mysteries or have adventures. But during the winter months Nubia likes to go to the baths, too. She's used to desert heat and says the only time she feels warm is in the hot, dry laconicum or the steamy sudatorium.

Pater usually goes out to dinner at

around four hours past noon. He dines with his patron or one of his friends. If he's out, Nubia and I have a light meal with Alma and Caudex.

Occasionally pater entertains and sometimes we are invited. We hardly ever recline – only at the Saturnalia or special family occasions. Pater thinks it's pretentious for children to recline. Instead, we sit at a table in the middle of the triclinium while the adults recline on couches around us.

We go to bed at sunset, or shortly after, which is nice in the summer but very frustrating in the winter. Alma says it's bad for my eyes, but sometimes I smuggle a scroll up to my bedroom and read by the light of my little clay oil-lamp. My favourite scroll at the moment is one by Apollodorus. He tells lots of Greek myths. I finally fall asleep and dream that I'm going on a quest or solving mysteries.

FESTIVALS AND HOLIDAYS

LMA always says 'life is brief' and pater explains that is why we celebrate so many festivals and holidays: to make sure the gods protect us and help us prosper. Why we make offerings to our household gods and also to Castor and Pollux, who are my family's patron deities.

Castor and Pollux are very popular here in Ostia, and they have a special festival called the Ludi Castorum at the end of January. These are games, and the highlight is a horse-race outside town near the salt-marshes.

In February we celebrate the Parentalia. That's when we bring out the painted wax death-masks of all our ancestors to pay them respect. On the last day of this festival I take flowers to the family tomb. If the weather's nice, we have a picnic there, near the ashes of my mother and twin brothers.

The Vulcanalia is one of the most exciting festivals. It takes place in August. Everyone has to throw a live fish on the coals as an offering to Vulcan, the smith god. He protects us against fire and flood. Last summer we celebrated the Vulcanalia on a beach south of Pompeii. The priest of Vulcan dropped the first fish – which is bad luck – and the next day a volcano called Vesuvius erupted! I will never forget that as long as I live!

Another festival is the Ludi Romani in September. It lasts nearly two weeks and up in Rome there are chariot races every day at the Circus

Maximus. We attended the races last year and it was one of the most exciting things I have ever witnessed. The chariots are so frail! And the horses go so fast!

The Saturnalia, near the end of December, is one of my favourite festivals. We take a five-day holiday from lessons and give gifts and have parties. Everything is upside-down. Our slaves recline and we serve them, instead of the other way round. We decorate the house with smiling garlands of evergreen plants and light lots of candles and oil lamps. Best of all, we all throw dice to choose the 'king of the Saturnalia'. I love being 'King of the Saturnalia' because I can tell everyone what to do!

Ceres – the goddess of grain – is also very important here in Ostia and we have celebrations for her three times a year. In fact, we Romans have so many festivals that I don't have enough room to list them all.

Apart from the big festivals, certain days are special. For example, every eight days is a market day. We call these days 'nundinae' because by our system of counting the market day itself is the ninth day. On those days farmers come in from out of town and sell their produce here in Ostia, or up in Rome. We used to divide the year into eight-day periods but since the time of Augustus we have started adopting the way of the east and are using a seven-day week, like Jonathan and his family.

There are also days called 'dies nefasti'. There are different types of these and it can get quite complicated. Basically, dies nefasti are days when the law-courts are closed and often the banks and markets, too. Sometimes they are ill-omened days when it's better to stay inside and not risk offending the gods.

The Kalends is what we call the first day of the month. Originally it was the day of the new moon, when the moon is the merest sliver of a crescent. The Nones used to mark the quarter moon and the Ides marked the full moon. The Ides are usually on the 13th or 15th day of the month. Usually odd-numbered days are lucky and even numbered days not. That's why pater will never set sail on an even day of the month.

My next-door-neighbour and friend Jonathan is Jewish, so his family celebrates different festivals. For example, every Friday night is special for them. They light candles and have a special Sabbath meal with a warm, plaited loaf of freshly baked bread. Sometimes they invite us.

Another festival they have is called 'Succot.' Each Jewish family builds a shelter of branches – called a succah – in their atrium or inner garden, under the open sky. For ten days, they eat and sleep there instead of in the proper rooms of their houses. They hang fruit from the roof of the succah and they make sure there are some spaces in the woven roof, so that they can see the stars overhead. Jonathan says it reminds his people of the time they wandered in the desert, before their god brought them into the Promised Land. It's so much fun eating and sleeping in the succah. At least for the first few days. Then I'm glad to get back to my own soft bed.

Gaius Plinius Caecilius Secundus, whom I call 'Younger Pliny', kindly gave me this list . . .

TOP FIVE REASONS FOR ESCAPING ROME IN THE SUMMER

1. The heat
2. The noise
3. The danger of pestilence or fever
4. The idle chatter and gossip of the lower classes who remain behind
5. The demands of people asking you to do them tedious favours, such as witnessing the signing of a will or attending a betrothal ceremony

Pliny's advice: *In the summer, don't linger in Rome; go to your Tuscan Villa or seaside retreat!*

MYTHS AND LEGENDS

I LOVE reading Greek myths, and Roman ones, too. Sometimes in lessons, our tutor Aristo lets us read a Greek or Latin text of one of the great epic poems like Homer's *Odyssey* or Virgil's *Aeneid*.

Hercules is a favourite hero of mine. Like most heroes, he is half god, half human. His father was Jupiter and his mother Alcmene. He was very strong and when just an infant he strangled two snakes with his chubby fists. Later – when he was grown-up – he strangled the Nemean lion! It was the first of twelve labours – or tasks – that he had to perform. Last year during the Saturnalia, something was troubling me: a kind of mystery. Hercules came to me in a dream and told me that if I completed twelve tasks based on his, then I would solve the mystery. It worked!

I also like the twin demi-gods Castor and Pollux. We call them the Gemini. Did you know that they were the brothers of Clytemnestra and her sister Helen of Troy? It's true. They were all four born from eggs! This is because their father Zeus (whom we Romans call Jupiter) came in the form of a swan when he met their mother Leda.

Poor Nubia gets confused sometimes because the Greek and Roman gods are almost identical and yet they have different names. For example, the goddess of love is Aphrodite in Greek, but Venus in Latin.

You can't escape myths and legends here in Ostia. They are painted on the frescoes of walls, depicted on the mosaics of floors and illustrated by statues and sculptures all over town. But I don't mind. I love the Greek myths and I will never tire of reading them.

TEN FAVOURITE GREEK MYTHS

It's strange, but all the mysteries I've solved seem to be linked to myths or legends. Here are some of my favourite myths and how they were linked to an adventure my friends and I shared.

1. PERSEUS AND MEDUSA

In this myth the hero Perseus had to find the monster Medusa and cut off her head. She was so ugly that one look at her turned people to stone. So Perseus used a sharp sword and a mirrored shield. One of the first mysteries I ever solved was who killed Jonathan's dog Bobas. The killer cut off Bobas's head, then put it in a bag, just like Perseus with Medusa!

2. VULCAN'S RETURN TO OLYMPUS

When we were in Pompeii last summer, we were searching for a 'treasure beyond imagining' and a blacksmith called Vulcan was the key. Of course that was only his nickname, but in many ways he was just like the god Vulcan, blacksmith to the gods.

3. DIONYSUS AND THE PIRATES

Did you know that the wine god Dionysus was once captured by pirates? He was clever and escaped using his powers. We were also captured by pirates last summer and we escaped using only our wits.

4. ODYSSEUS ESCAPES FROM THE CYCLOPS

I have always loved Homer's *Odyssey*. It is the story of the Greek hero Odysseus and his long voyage home from Troy. He is very clever and eludes many monsters. The scariest monster is the Cyclops, a man-eating giant with one huge eye in the middle of his forehead. When Jonathan disappeared to Rome last year, we discovered him in Nero's Golden House, in a room called the Cyclops' Cave.

5. ARION AND THE DOLPHIN

Arion was the handsome young king of Corinth in Greece, where our tutor Aristo comes from. He played the lyre beautifully, just like Aristo. Arion went to Sicily for a musical competition and won lots of gold. On his way home the sailors wanted to kill him and steal his gold. Arion tried playing music to soften their hearts. His music did not affect the cruel sailors but it did attract some dolphins. When Arion jumped overboard to escape the murderous sailors, one dolphin carried him all the way home to

Corinth! You might say it's only a myth, but I have actually seen a person riding a dolphin – Lupus!

6. THE TWELVE TASKS OF HERCULES

Hercules is a strange hero. He is very brave and strong, but sometimes he does foolish things. One day he got drunk and killed his family. As atonement he had to complete twelve 'impossible tasks' or labours. During the Saturnalia last year I had a mystery to solve. One day Hercules came to me in a dream. He told me that if I performed twelve tasks like his, I would solve the mystery. And it worked!

7. PROMETHEUS AND PANDORA

Prometheus was immortal. He brought fire to mankind. Jupiter became angry and punished him by making a vulture peck his liver all day. But Prometheus couldn't die, and his liver grew back every night and then the vulture came again in the morning. So his torment was never-ending. According to some, Pandora was the sister of Prometheus. She opened a box filled with all kinds of illness and disease. I think of these two

when I think of the terrible fire and plague that Rome has just suffered.

8. ORPHEUS AND EURYDICE

So many of the Greek myths are very sad. But they are also beautiful. The musician Orpheus lost his beloved wife Eurydice on the very day of their wedding. She was bitten by a snake and she died and went down to the underworld. Orpheus followed and tried to save her. I won't spoil the ending, but it's very sad.

9. PEGASUS THE FLYING HORSE

I would love to be able to fly high above the earth and look down on it. Wouldn't that be wonderful? If I had a flying horse like Pegasus, then I could do that. I would so love a flying horse.

10. DIANA AND HER HUNTRESSES

Diana is one of my favourite goddesses. She isn't bothered about men and marriage and babies. She just wants to run free with her friends and have adventures and hunt her prey. Is it any wonder she is my favourite goddess?

CAPTAIN GEMINUS

FULL NAME: Marcus Flavius Gai filius Voturia tribu Geminus

BIRTHDAY: 24 May AD 48

BIRTHPLACE: Stabia (near Pompeii)

EYE COLOUR: Blue-grey

HAIR COLOUR: Light brown (flavus means 'tawny')

FAVOURITE FOOD: Grilled sole with parsley and lemon

FAVOURITE PLACE: At the tiller of my ship on a fine day

FAVOURITE TIME OF DAY: Sunset, dropping anchor in a secluded cove

TOPICS ASSIGNED BY FLAVIA: Transport and Trade, Patrons and Clients

You have asked me, Flavia, to write a few words describing my childhood and how I became a sea captain. I am not quite certain who your intended audience is, so I'll keep it short and simple.

Your great grandfather, Marcus Flavius Salinator of the tribe of Voturia, was a salt-trader here in Ostia. However, his wife came from Campania, and when he made his fortune they moved to Stabia and bought a large farm with vineyards and olive groves. My father – Gaius Flavius Agricola – married a girl of the equestrian class named Julia and they lived with my grandparents on the farm. That is where your Uncle Gaius and I were born. A few years later, our younger sisters Flavia Agricola and Flavilla were born. We all had a very happy childhood. My father had a good bailiff, who managed the farm so efficiently that my father had time to teach us in the mornings. He was very forward-thinking and he included our little sisters in lessons, until their untimely death in the seventh year of Nero.

Although I am ten minutes younger than Gaius, I was always the more adventurous one. Gaius loved plants and animals, and he was always in the garden pottering about with seedlings. I loved reading about exotic lands and could usually be found in my father's extensive library. Whenever pater went into Pompeii on market-days, I would beg to go, too. Once there, I would make my way to the port and watch the ships depart and arrive. One day – I shall never forget it – I saw a ship dock and watched them unloading wild-beasts from Libya. I remember there were lions, antelope and a camelopard! The sight of them! The smell! The sound! I have never been so excited in my life, and I vowed that when I was grown up, I would have a ship of my own and travel the world.

As you know, my mother Julia died giving birth to twins – as your own mother did – when Gaius and I were twelve years old. A fever took our two younger sisters and grandparents the following year. There was a bad quake in the region the year after that, when Gaius and I were about fourteen. Your grandfather was hit on the head by a heavy beam in one of the outbuildings.

He never recovered from that blow – or from the loss of his wife, parents and daughters – and he died a broken man a few years later, not long after Gaius and I assumed the toga virilis. In his will, my father left Gaius the farm and me enough money to buy a ship. We were both well satisfied with this, I the more so because I was courting your mother and she longed to travel just as I did. Naming my ship after her was an inspiration. She agreed to marry me, and so I acquired two precious Myrtillas. Your mother and my ship.

Sadly the gods have seen fit to take them both from me, but I have a consolation in you, my dearest daughter. I pray that one day you will marry and present me with half a dozen strong young grandsons to carry on the family line. Perhaps there will be a future farmer or ship's captain among them.

TRANSPORT AND TRADE

Your suggestion that I write a few words on transport and trade is a welcome one. I'm delighted that you want to know more about a subject so dear to me.

Roman roads, built by legionary soldiers, are the best in the world. They are straight and true, and designed to shed water and provide rapid communication between provinces. Mule- or ox-carts transport goods around Italia. They carry everything from blocks of marble to fresh oysters in barrels of sea-water. Fast horses carry the imperial messengers from one post to the next. The reason you often see them riding on the dirt path beside the road – rather than on the road itself – is because that surface is easier on their hooves and they can gallop. The roads are mainly travelled by pedestrians and carts, as you can tell by the deep wheel ruts carved over time.

You have to be wary of robbers, especially as you reach the outskirts of a city. They tend to hide among the tombs just outside the city walls. But apart from the odd robber or broken wheel, land transport is efficient and quick in our great Empire.

However, it's no match for the amount of territory you can cover at sea.

We Romans are not natural seafarers, like the Phoenicians. In fact some have called us landlubbers. But that has not stopped us taking advantage of the great sea routes.

For example, most of the bread eaten here in Italia is made from African grain. Every year the grain arrives on huge transport ships from Carthage, Leptis Magna and especially Alexandria. These massive grain ships dock in Puteoli, the great commercial port near Neapolis, or in Portus, the new harbour just a few miles north of here. (We often see them passing by.) From Portus, the wheat is carried by barge up the River Tiber to Rome, or it is stored here in the great granaries of Ostia. Grain is Ostia's lifeblood, you know, hence the number of granaries, bakeries and measurer's guilds.

Ours may be a smaller and older harbour than the one up at Portus, but it also serves Rome well. You can still find many exotic goods here in the Marina Forum: silk from the Indies, spices from Asia, garum and olive oil from Hispania, lead from Britannia, wine from Massilia, gum mastic from Chios, ivory from Africa, glassware from Alexandria and perfume from Rhodes. We also have the so-called Forum of the Corporations here. This is where those guilds connected with trade and sailing meet. The guilds of shipping-agents, wild-beast importers and sail-makers all have offices there, with mosaics out front to show their specialty. My corporation – that of sea-captains – has an office there, too. Whenever I need a new crewmember I just post a notice there and applicants come to see me.

Sea-travel is efficient, but dangerous. As you know, I recently lost my beloved ship, and almost my life, in a terrifying way.

It happened last August, just after the eruption of Vesuvius (although we did not know that at the time). We had left the port of Alexandria with a full cargo of spices and had begun the run to Crete. That's one of the most dangerous parts of the voyage, because it's across open water. Suddenly, without warning, an enormous wave was upon us, like a cliff of green glass. It struck the *Myrtilla* amidships. One moment my ship was beneath us, the next she was gone. I was washed up onto a rocky island, the only survivor as far as I knew. At last, I was rescued by a Syrian merchant ship bound for Rome. When I finally reached Ostia, I cut off my hair and dedicated it as a thanks offering at the Temple of Neptune.

Now I intend to captain another vessel called the *Delphina*, an ex-slave-ship. I am working to refurbish her, and when she is seaworthy I intend to sacrifice an entire bull for the 'lustratio', the purification ceremony. It will be very expensive but I cannot risk offending the gods.

CAPTAIN GEMINUS'S TOP FIVE TIPS FOR TRAVELLING BY SEA

1. There are no ships just for passengers, so you'll have to find a merchant ship – or one of the big grain ships – travelling to your destination. Ask the captain if you can pay for deck space. But choose your man carefully; some unscrupulous captains take on passengers then rob them and toss them overboard when they're out at sea!

2. Take your own food supply and a slave to prepare it; most captains won't let you mess with their crew. And don't forget a bedroll and waterproof cloak.

3. Always make an offering to Neptune before you go and make sure to give him a thanks offering when you arrive safely.

4. For seasickness, drink seawater. It will make you vomit, but then you'll feel much better.

5. Things you must never do on a ship: step onto the deck with your left foot, sneeze or cut your hair. Never embark on an even day, and never sail between the months of November and March; it's not unlucky, it's suicide!

PATRONS AND CLIENTS

Almost every man in the Roman Empire has at least one patron. All except for the Emperor. He is the Patron of all. A patron is a man of power or wealth who has people who are dependent on him in some way. He helps them, and in return they do favours for him. The relationship can be as simple as the ex-master whose freedman has set up a small business, or more complicated. Before the destruction of his farm, my brother Gaius was the patron of his own freedmen and tenant farmers, but had several patrons of his own.

Most patrons prefer their clients to visit them first thing in the morning. This early-morning visit is called the 'salutatio'. Patrons hear requests at that time, but they will also ask their clients to perform certain favours in return, like coming along to support them plead a case in court, or applauding at a reading of their poetry, or even voting for them in elections. In return, the patron gives his client a small amount of money, or sometimes a basket of goodies, called a 'sportula'. Some patrons do not give this sportula but repay their clients by inviting them to dinner parties. This is how my patron Cordius treats his clients. His parties are delightful, but some patrons are very stingy.

Whenever Cordius is in Ostia, and I am not at sea, I attend his salutatio. For that reason, my own clients rarely find me at home first thing in the morning. But they know I can be found at my office in the Forum of the Corporations from mid-morning, after I've been to the barber.

This is your reward for cutting short your sleep and rushing out every morning with your sandals undone: your patron's dinner! The wine is so bad even new wool won't absorb it . . . The bread is so hard you can't bite into it without breaking your teeth. And yet your patron chews soft white bread made of the finest flour.
Juvenal on patrons repaying clients with a meal (from Satires 5.12ff)

UNCLE GAIUS

FULL NAME: Gaius Flavius G. f. Vot. Geminus

BIRTHDAY: 24 May AD 48

BIRTHPLACE: Stabia (near Pompeii)

EYE COLOUR: Blue-grey

HAIR COLOUR: Light brown (flavus means 'tawny')

FAVOURITE FOOD: Any meal made from the produce of my own farm

FAVOURITE PLACE: Walking in my vineyards

FAVOURITE TIME OF DAY: Early morning when all is peaceful

TOPIC ASSIGNED BY FLAVIA: Farming and Agriculture

Greetings, dear niece. My brother tells me you have also asked him to write an account of his childhood. Although Marcus and I are identical in looks, we are quite different in nature. It will be interesting to see how our memories differ, don't you think?

As you know, we are twins. I am older by about ten minutes.

When I was about four years old, I fell out of the old fig tree which used to stand on the edge of the vineyards of my Stabian farm. You remember it; you and your friends built a treehouse in it last summer. It was ancient back then, nearly thirty years ago. Marcus and I were competing to see who could climb highest and fastest. I was ahead when I put my foot on a rotten branch. It broke and I fell to the ground. I seemed to fall for ever, striking one branch after another. Perhaps hitting all those branches on the way down saved my life, but I was bruised from head to toe, and broke my left leg. I stayed in bed for a month recovering and then recuperated by helping mater tend the inner garden. By the time I regained full movement I had gained a deep love for plants and growing things. And the next time Marcus challenged me to climb a tree I realised I had lost my nerve.

I believe that old fig tree is the reason Marcus became a sea-captain and I became a farmer. When my father died, Marcus was happy for me to keep the farm as long as I gave him enough funds to buy his ship. Nobody could have foreseen the terrible disaster a dozen years later that took my farm from me and his ship from him.

Many men of my class let their bailiffs do all the work while they write poetry or hunt with their friends. But I used to love taking part in the day-to-day activity of the farm. I knew the names of all my field slaves and the names of the goats and sheep as well.

Every day I would rise at cockcrow and make an offering to my household gods. Then, I would walk out between the vine-rows and think about the day ahead. As dawn broke, the farm came alive: goats bleated, chickens clucked, and slaves laughed or grumbled, depending on their temperament.

One day I would help attend the

birthing of a lamb. Another I would oversee the pressing of olives. Last summer there were many earth tremors and some of the outbuildings needed repairs. I didn't know it then but those tremors were prophesying the eruption of Vesuvius. Even if I had known, there is nothing I could have done to prevent the total destruction of the farm that had been in my family for three generations.

I now rent a small lodge near Laurentum, on the estate of young Pliny. It has a small vineyard and a few olives, and there is a little rose garden at the back of the house. Having been a rich landowner for many years, I am now reduced to being a tenant farmer, and the client of a youth half my age. But I have the most beautiful wife in the world, so I suppose the gods have not totally abandoned me.

FARMING AND AGRICULTURE

I THINK it must be every Roman's dream to have a farm in the country, far from the heat and stench and bustle of town. Horace the poet was overjoyed when his patron Maecenas gave him a little farm with its own natural spring of cold water. And I was thrilled when my father left me his property in his will.

Columella says farms should be divided into three sections: living quarters for the owner and his family; stalls for the slaves and animals; and a third section for storage and farm works such as the threshing floor or wine-press. That is how my grandfather arranged our Stabian farm and it worked very well.

In the living quarters we had two dining rooms, a small bathhouse and even a library (my father was quite a scholar). There was a basic bathhouse near the slaves' quarters, too, for Columella recommends that slaves should be allowed to bathe, if only on holidays. (I prefer Columella's advice on slaves to that of Cato, who treated his slaves worse than his livestock.)

We had stables for the animals, a pen for goats, and a coop for the chickens. There was also an oil-press, a grape-press and room where the wine matured in barrels, before being transferred to amphoras. The wine produced by my vines was famous and I was very proud of it. One of my patrons, Pollius Felix, used to buy the bulk of it. It was a useful and steady income.

The soil around Stabia was very rich. I know now that this must have been because it was volcanic soil from Vesuvius. But until last August, nobody suspected that mountain was a dormant volcano. That is why the richest landowners had villas up there. I recall now that on several occasions the smell of sulphur was reported on its upper slopes.

If only I had heeded the signs! But even so, what could I have done except abandon my farm and move away? Ruin was inevitable.

Grain is packed down in every corner and the amphoras of wine smell of fine vintages . . . Here, when November is over and winter on its way, the shaggy vine-pruner is still bringing home late bunches of grapes . . . The greedy pigs follow the bailiff's wife with her full apron . . . Farm children sit around the crackling fire . . . and a rustic neighbour brings honey on the comb and a cone of milk . . .

Martial on the farm of his friend Faustinus
(Epigrams 3.58.5 passim)

JONATHAN

FULL NAME: Jonathan ben Mordecai

BIRTHDAY: 15 September AD 68

ELEMENT: Earth

BIRTHPLACE: Jerusalem in Judaea

EYE COLOUR: Dark brown

HAIR COLOUR: Brown and curly

FAVOURITE FOOD: Venison stew and anything with honey

FAVOURITE PLACE: Hunting in the woods with my dog Tigris

FAVOURITE TIME OF DAY: Early autumn mornings, best for hunting

TOPICS ASSIGNED BY FLAVIA: Sport and Entertainment, Religion

So, Flavia, you want me to write something about myself? I was born in Jerusalem about a year and a half before Titus marched on it with four legions. He plundered our Holy Temple, destroyed Jerusalem and either killed or enslaved its inhabitants. My father Mordecai and my older sister Miriam and I got out in time. But my mother was left behind. So I grew up without her.

Over the centuries we Jews have suffered persecution from almost everybody, especially the Romans. My family also follows 'The Way', a new sect whose believers are persecuted by Jews. So we are the most perse-cuted of the persecuted.

We lived in Rome for a while, then moved to the Jewish quarter in Ostia, to be near my aunt and other relatives. But the Jews there disapproved of my father's beliefs. Some of them pelted us with rotten cabbages. Others wrote graffiti on the wall of our house telling us to get out, so we had to move again. That's when we moved next door to you, Flavia. About a week after we moved in, our dog Bobas was killed. His head was chopped off. You helped me solve the mystery and we caught the culprit. But that didn't bring Bobas back.

Since then I almost died in the eruption of Vesuvius, was captured by pirates, got branded on the arm and accidentally started a fire that killed twenty thousand people up in Rome.

Once you called me a pessimist, Flavia. Can you really blame me?

SPORT AND ENTERTAINMENT

So you want me to entertain you by talking about entertainment? Don't I get enough homework from Aristo?

THE BATHS

Romans like the baths more than almost anything else. After a long morning's work at the forum or in school, it's good to hear the gongs clanging noon, announcing the opening of the baths. After a light lunch you can go along and strip off your clothes in the changing room, rub down with oil, then have a good workout in the palaestra. I was getting fat last year but have vowed to get fit. So I run and lift weights. When I'm all hot and sweaty I go into the caldarium or the sudatorium and let the steam loosen the dirt and sweat. I scrape it off with my bronze strigil, then have a good long swim in the outdoor swimming pool. Lupus is usually there already. He loves swimming. After our swim, if I'm still stiff I'll pay a few sesterces for a massage with scented oil. I lie on a cool marble slab in a room decorated with frescos and mosaics and let a slave work out the kinks in my muscles. Not bad. Then I'll wrap a linen towel around myself and go lie in the solarium. Maybe have a little doze, if it's a hot, sultry afternoon, or chat with Lupus or even play a board game with him. Some time between the third and fourth hour after noon – when the day starts to cool down – we'll get up and get dressed and walk slowly back home, clean and relaxed and refreshed.

CHARIOT RACES

Of the various types of big public entertainment, the chariot races are probably the most popular with the Romans. With me too, I have to admit. The Circus Maximus up in Rome seats a quarter of a million people. I remember the first time I went. When the chariots appeared through the archway at the far end of the racecourse for their procession, I could not believe the roar that went up. It seemed as if the whole world was there cheering. The most exciting races are those with four-horse chariots, or quadrigae. Four ungelded stallions pull a man — sometimes a boy — on a chariot that is little more than a basket on wheels. They go unbelievably fast, throwing up a spray of sand as they round the turning points. The charioteers tie the leather reins round their waist, to leave their hands free to twitch a particular rein or wield the whip. But that means that if they are thrown out of their chariot then they are dragged along the racetrack until they can cut themselves free. They actually keep a sharp knife in their belts for this very purpose, but sometimes they're not fast enough and get trampled by another quadriga. It's horrible to see and I can hardly watch, but the constant threat of that happening is what makes your heart pound when the race is on.

BEAST FIGHTS

If you go to the arena on a festival day, the morning's events will mainly be beast-fights. They'll start with a mass of exotic herbivores like giraffes and antelope being hunted by carnivores like starved lions and bears. Then they send in the beast-hunters to kill off the carnivores with bow and arrow or javelin. Sometimes they put on a single combat between two wild animals. For example, a bear against a bull. Because animals set loose in the amphitheatre won't just naturally attack each other, slaves prod the animals with red-hot irons to drive them mad with pain. Then they'll attack each other. Or sometimes they chain the two animals together, to make them fight. I hunt animals and I'm not squeamish about killing them for food, but I can't bear to watch the beast fights. They're just cruel and barbaric.

EXECUTION OF CRIMINALS

During the lunch break — between the beast fights and the gladiatorial combats — the Romans sometimes execute criminals. They do it publicly, in order to discourage others from committing similar crimes. But they don't just chop off the heads of the criminals. Oh, no. The Romans execute them in 'entertaining and educational' ways. Aristo once told me about a man who robbed a temple. They dressed him up as Icarus in a loincloth and curly wig, and they even tied on little wings made of wax and feathers. Then they hauled him up above the arena on a kind of harness and dropped him from a great height. People were shouting, 'Fly, Icarus! Fly!' But he obviously didn't fly. Aristo said the worst thing was that the fall didn't kill him so they had a slave dressed as Pluto come out and bash him on the head with a mallet. In all fairness, not every Roman likes these executions. You know that one of my favourite philosophers is Seneca. He wrote about how awful the lunchtime executions were. I agree with him.

GLADIATORIAL COMBATS

Men fighting against men. Sometimes to the death. Whoever thought this up? It's the main event of a day at the arena. In the early afternoon, the gladiators come out all together to salute the crowds and the emperor. Their weapons are tested for sharpness, then they fight in carefully controlled pairs, while a referee watches. The Romans have managed to pair differently-armed types of gladiators. For example, the Retiarius – unprotected apart from a shoulder

guard and armed with no more than a trident and net – usually fights the Secutor, whose tight smooth helmet deflects the deadly points of the trident. Or a Thracian might fight a Murmillo; the Thracian's curved sword can sneak round the edge of the Murmillo's big rectangular shield. Even though the gladiators are evenly paired, matches rarely last more than a quarter of an hour. If a gladiator is badly wounded or pinned down by his opponent, he holds up a forefinger to ask for mercy. The referee stops the fight and all three of them look to the editor, the man who has paid for the games. The editor – usually the emperor or a rich candidate for office – looks around to see what the crowd wants. If the defeated gladiator fought well, the plebs usually wave handkerchiefs to show they want him spared. If the loser fought poorly, they give the thumbs-down, to show he should be executed. The decision is up to the editor, but he usually does what the crowd wants. After all, that's the point of the games: to win favour with as many people as possible.

HUNTING

The pastime of many aristocratic Romans – who don't have to work for a living – is hunting. That is my favourite pastime, too. You know how much I like hunting in the pinewoods here in Ostia. I hunt with my bow and arrow or my sling, sometimes both. I prefer hunting by myself – with Tigris, of course – but sometimes hunting with others can be interesting. In a proper hunting-party, slaves go out the day before and tie nets to trees. They attach dyed birds' feathers to the edge of the nets. The red feathers flutter in the breeze and drive animals into the centre. On the day of the hunt, the master sends his beaters ahead. They drive any big animals into the nets. Then you go in with spears, javelins or bow to kill off the animals. Remember the time Aristo and his friend and Lupus and I helped kill an escaped ostrich in the pine woods right here in Ostia? That was exciting.

GAMBLING AND DICING

Lupus should be telling you about this. He's the one with his own dice, shaved, of course. People bet on horses in the chariot races and on gladiators in the arena. Of course, it's illegal to gamble or to roll dice any time except the Saturnalia, but you and I know it goes on all the time.

ATTENDING READINGS

A 'reading', as you know, is when a poet reads some of his own work to a gathering of friends and clients. Remember that reading we went to last month? Where Pliny was reading excerpts from a Greek tragedy he wrote when he was fourteen. I thought it was going to be really boring. It was.

MIME

You often see mime troupes performing on makeshift stages around the town, or even in a portico of the

forum. Afterwards, one of them passes round an upturned tambourine and if you enjoyed the show, you drop in your coin. But they also perform in the theatre for certain festivals. My father says mime is the lowest form of theatrical entertainment. The actors are sometimes women or girls who strip off their clothes. The men make crude gestures and wear rude props. The language is obscene. The stories are usually about ordinary people and their faults: lust, greed, envy, deception. The crowds love it.

PANTOMIME

Pantomime is a much higher form of entertainment than mime. In pantomime, one actor dances all the parts of a story, usually from Greek mythology. The dancer wears a mask — or a succession of masks — but unlike comedy and tragedy the masks have closed mouths because the dancer never speaks. Instead, a singer in his troupe sings the story to the accompaniment of his musicians. Remember Aristo was telling us about that young pantomime dancer up in Rome? His name is Paris and everyone says he's going to be a star.

TRAGEDY

We know all about tragedy because we've been studying Greek tragedies with Aristo this past year. They usually involve mythological characters and have terrible endings where everyone is left either dead or devastated. What fun.

COMEDY

I saw part of a comedy when we lived in Rome. I remember it had a wily slave who wanted to buy his freedom, a stupid father, a domineering mother and a young son who was in love with an unsuitable girl who turned out to be suitable after all. Father told me that most comedies by Roman playwrights have fairly similar plots. That one was by Plautus, who lived about 300 years ago. I have to admit, it was still funny, three centuries later.

Of course, most of these types of entertainment are put on as part of your festivals, to honour the Roman gods. We Jews do not have festivals like that, but it doesn't stop us enjoying your Roman ones.

RELIGION

We Jews read Torah and observe the Sabbath. But my father follows the teachings of a rabbi who claimed to be our Messiah, the anointed one. His name was Yeshua (or 'Jesus' as they call him here). He taught for a few years in Judaea. Then – about fifty years ago – he allowed them to crucify him. But after three days he came back from the dead and is sitting at the right hand of God. He offers those who believe in him eternal life in paradise. We believe that he will come again any day to usher in his Kingdom. We also believe that he sent his Spirit to help us while we are still here on earth. Our sect is called 'The Way'.

For various reasons my father lets us eat any food now – except food that he knows was sacrificed to one of your gods. Remember the first time I had dinner at your house and you served snails? I'd never tried them before, but my father said it was permitted. So I tried them. And I liked them. Also, we are not as strict about the Sabbath as we used to be. Father says, 'The Sabbath was created for Man,' and he lets me hunt and Miriam weave and sometimes he even sees his patients. But we still observe the Sabbath by lighting the candles and having our special meal and not having lessons with Aristo, as you know! We celebrate the day of our Messiah's

The Temple to Jupiter

resurrection on the morning after the Sabbath. Some people call us Christians, because the word for Messiah in Greek is Christ. There are more Christians here in Ostia than you might think, but they mostly keep it secret. Under the reign of

Nero our sect was badly persecuted, and many people think it could easily happen again.

But Romans are fairly tolerant. Lots of you worship some of the new eastern gods, like Isis from Egypt and Mithras from Persia. I suppose you have so many gods in your pantheon that a couple more don't matter.

You Romans call us atheists, because we don't acknowledge other gods, and we refuse to worship deified men like the dead emperors of Rome. Also, we Jews don't sacrifice animals any more. We used to, but then ten years ago Titus destroyed the great Temple in Jerusalem and from that day all sacrifices stopped. Father says it doesn't matter, because our Messiah was a sacrifice once and for all. So we don't need the Temple any more.

JONATHAN'S TOP FIVE TIPS FOR HUNTING

1. Train your dog to obey your commands instantly. An ill-trained dog can startle a rabbit or bird too soon.

2. Early morning is the best time of the day to hunt, and autumn the best season of the year.

3. Sticky yellow birdlime is useful for trapping little birds. Smear it on a rod and hold it up high where birds settle. Once they've landed they won't be able to fly away. Then you can just snap their necks.

4. Practise every day with your bow and arrow (or your sling). If you miss even one day you start to get rusty. And that can make the difference between venison stew for dinner or yesterday's leftover barley porridge.

5. If you don't have a bow or sling, a throwing stick can stun a hare long enough for you to approach it and break its neck.

DOCTOR MORDECAI

FULL NAME: Mordecai ben Ezra

BIRTHDAY: 11 February AD 37

BIRTHPLACE: Babylon in Babylonia

EYE COLOUR: Dark brown

HAIR COLOUR: Brown

FAVOURITE FOOD: Roast lamb

FAVOURITE PLACE: Reading Torah in my study

FAVOURITE TIME OF DAY: Friday evening, the start of the Sabbath

TOPICS ASSIGNED BY FLAVIA: Medicine, Death and Burial

I WAS born in Babylon. My father was a doctor. And his father before him. From an early age I wanted to follow in their footsteps.

I remember my grandfather well. He was a great scholar, and knew the Torah better than anyone I have ever met. He practised medicine all week, and then on the Sabbath he would meet with his friends and discuss Torah all day. I used to sit on his lap and stroke his long white beard. His eyes were full of intelligence and wit. I adored him. When I was seventeen, my father and I travelled to the great city of Alexandria. My father found me a place at the Mouseion, and saw me established an apprentice to his friend Judas, a surgeon of great modesty and wisdom. My father returned to Babylon and for several years I helped Jonah in his afternoon rounds, attending classes in the mornings. It was there at the Mouseion that I saw my first corpse dissected. It was an extraordinary and

rare experience. In my life I have only seen half a dozen dissections – all in Alexandria – but I can remember every one in detail. It has helped me to operate on living bodies and it has convinced me that the arteries are not filled with air – as most doctors claim – but with blood, just as the veins are.

It was during my fifth year in Alexandria that a fever swept through the Jewish community back in Babylon. It took everyone in the family except my two elder sisters, who decided to move to Jerusalem. Some years later I followed, and set up practice in that beautiful city. I felt I had come home.

It was there in Jerusalem that I met a man called Jacob, who taught me about 'The Way'. It was also in Jerusalem that I met Susannah, the love of my life. We had two wonderful children, Miriam and Jonathan. For all those reasons, Jerusalem will always be golden to me. Even though it lies devastated and in ruins.

MEDICINE

As you know, Flavia, the body is composed of four main substances and each of us tends to have a surfeit of one of them. You, for example, are 'sanguine'. This means you tend to have too much blood. You sanguine types often have pink cheeks and tend to flush easily. You are naturally optimistic and cheerful, but you also have short tempers. You are quick at making decisions, even impetuous. Do you not agree that this is a perfect description of you?

Cosmus the doctor with Flavia

Lupus is phlegmatic. His body has a tendency to produce too much phlegm or mucus. Phlegm makes a person brave, so phlegmatic types tend to be impetuous. They also have strong mood swings, up one moment and down the next. And they are stoical about pain.

Choleric people have too much yellow bile. They can be anxious or irritable. Nubia is rarely irritable, but she is often anxious and for that reason I suspect she is choleric.

My own Jonathan is the classic melancholic. His spleen produces too much black bile. They tend to be pessimists and often carry the weight of the world on their shoulders.

For an excess of one of the humours I prescribe either 'dry cupping' or 'wet cupping'. In dry cupping I take my bleeding cup and put a piece of flaming lint inside. Immediately I press it to the patient's back. The flame goes out and causes a sucking sensation. This sucking removes excess of one of the humours, which are not in themselves bad.

Wet cupping is also known as bleeding. For this I make a small incision with a sharp scalpel, usually in the crook of the elbow or in the wrist, and I take a cupful of the patient's blood. This is a good remedy for anxiety and stress, but should never be used for faintness or loss of blood, as some doctors do.

Here in the Roman Empire, anyone can practise medicine. Having visited the infirmary on the Tiber Island, you know as well as I do that some so-called doctors should be in another profession altogether. Diaulus, in particular, would do better as an undertaker since he kills most of his patients anyway. Bleeding can be good in some cases, but that man bleeds them dry. Cosmus was the best of the lot, though to my mind he should run a perfume shop with that nose of his. As to Egnatius, the doctor who advises his patients to drink their own urine, even he is better than Diaulus.

Many of the best doctors of the past have been Greek: Hippocrates, for example, the 'father of medicine'. He wrote the oath we still take today. And he said 'Food is medicine.'

Mind you, it depends on the dose. A tincture of hellebore can be used to calm hysteria in women, but too much will cause vomiting, diarrhoea and eventually death.

Herbs and other medicines are very important in my profession. Some of them I collect myself, but most I buy from the apothecary here in Ostia. I keep a selection of the most useful herbs in my capsa – a cylindrical leather carrying case. I also keep my basic instruments there: a scalpel, tweezers, probe and bleeding cup. Sometimes I go out to patients, but mostly they call here in the mornings, like any client calling on his patron. I suppose in a way, I am a patron of the sick!

Asclepiades, another very practical Greek physician, proposed five simple principles for curing minor ailments.

In fact, many of those who are ill or infirm will recover if they are simply left alone. As the great Hippocrates wisely said, 'The gods are the real physicians, though people do not think so.' What he means is that if you make the patient comfortable and at ease, they will often recover with no other treatment.

Diaulus was recently a doctor.
Now he is an undertaker.
What he now does as an undertaker
he used to do as a doctor!
Martial (Epigrams I.47)

Asclepiades was a doctor credited by many for establishing Greek medicine in Rome. He lived nearly two hundred years ago, but his excellent principles still apply.

ASCLEPIADES' TOP FIVE PRINCIPLES FOR TREATING MINOR AILMENTS

1. Fasting (no food)
2. Abstinence (no wine)
3. Walking
4. Rocking (in a cart or carriage)
5. Massage

DEATH AND BURIAL

Did you know, Flavia, that we Jews never burn our dead? We anoint the body with balm or scented oil, wrap it in linen strips and place it in a tomb, sepulchre or grave.

You Romans favour cremation, when the body is burned on a pyre. Then the bones are washed and placed in urns along with the ashes. The fire does not destroy everything and I have always thought it must be a terrible thing for a father to have to wash the bones of his children, or a young wife the bones of her husband.

Forgive me for saying it, but I believe you Romans revere your dead too much. We Jews respect our ancestors, and will not disturb their bones, but we do not keep wax masks of them in our vestibules, nor do we visit their graves to 'dine' with them. However, like you Romans, we do not permit our dead to be buried within the city walls.

As a doctor I know that 'life is short'. At any moment an infected cut or sudden fever can carry us away. Even though I believe in eternal life after this one, I dream of a day when medicine will give people a longer life-expectancy than thirty. I dream of a day when town and country will be full of many greyheads, rather than just a few. And I dream of a day when young girls will not fear giving birth and when babies will thrive and be healthy and grow to realise their full potential.

Stranger, I have a little tale to tell, stand by and read it through. This is the ugly tomb of a beautiful woman. Her parents named her Claudia. She loved her husband with all her heart. She bore two sons. One of these she leaves on earth. The other she has placed under the earth. She was charming in her speech, but modest in her manner. She managed the household. She spun wool. I have spoken. Farewell.

Epitaph from a Roman tomb (Corpus of Latin Inscriptions VI I5346)

MIRIAM

FULL NAME: Miriam bat Mordecai

BIRTHDAY: 15 July AD 65

BIRTHPLACE: Jerusalem in Judaea

EYE COLOUR: Violet

HAIR COLOUR: Black, glossy and curly

FAVOURITE FOOD: Fresh figs or grapes

FAVOURITE PLACE: A peaceful garden

FAVOURITE TIME OF DAY: Early morning, everything still sparkling with dew

TOPIC ASSIGNED BY FLAVIA: Love and Marriage

I hate being beautiful. Everyone says I am lucky to be so lovely. But it is a curse. Men want to possess me, as if I was some kind of trophy, and women envy me. And because of my beauty, people stare at me. Sometimes their bold looks prick me like hairpins. I want to pull my palla over my head and run away.

I am happiest with my family and friends. To them my beauty is invisible because they know me for who I am: sometimes irritable, often impatient and not very clever or witty. But they love me and I am happy in that knowledge.

I was born in Jerusalem and have only a few memories of that city. One is of playing with my friend Hephzibah in our tiled courtyard. The other is of my mother and father standing on the upper roof of our house, speaking softly together. My mother Susannah was only fifteen when she married my father. He was twice her age. She gave birth to me a year later. When I was little I thought fifteen very grown-up but now that I am that age I think it is really quite young.

For many years, I had to perform the chores of a mother, cook and seamstress.

I didn't mind too much. I love cooking and sewing.

A few years ago I began helping my father when he went to attend women in childbirth. It is such a miraculous thing, when a baby comes into the world. I always praise God when a baby is born, and I can never help crying.

My favourite occupation is walking in a garden. I love to watch plants grow from tiny tender sprouts to fruit bearing trees. And I love flowers, their texture, their fragrance and their cool blossoms.

Now that I am married, I have my own little rose garden. It is bliss. Over the next few years, I hope to fill it with happy, laughing children. For me, that will be paradise.

LOVE AND MARRIAGE

What can I say about love and marriage? Father used to tell me he would arrange a suitable marriage for me and I was happy to obey. But then I met your uncle, and fell in love with him. Thank goodness father agreed to the match, even though he says I am very young. I have to remind him that mother was also fifteen when he married her!

Because Gaius is Roman, our wedding was a mixture of Jewish and Roman customs.

In a Roman wedding, they part the bride's hair with the sharp point of a spear! The crowds shout rude jokes as the bride goes in procession to the house of her husband-to-be. Luckily she wears a saffon-coloured veil to hide her blushes. Boys pelt her with nuts and musicians play a frantic tune that sets your pulse racing.

Our Jewish weddings are not so terrifying. The bride's hair is plaited with pearls or gold, not parted with a spear. The bridegroom comes to collect his bride and instead of tearing her from her mother's arms, he receives her parents' blessing. They then proceed together to his house by torchlight. Instead of being pelted with nuts, the people lining the route scatter ears of parched grain. Instead of bawdy jokes there are songs of joy. At the bridegroom's house, the bride is led to stand quietly under a canopy in the courtyard to be blessed by an elder. Then there is a feast with drinking and the posing of riddles, like the one Samson put to his bridegrooms. Finally the husband goes to his wife as the guests feast downstairs.

My wedding was a blend of the two.

The betrothal ceremony was very Jewish, with all our relatives there to witness the giving of the ring, and me dressed in my headdress of gold coins. So was the Day of Henna, when all my female friends came to gossip and nibble sweetmeats while the henna was applied to my hands and feet.

But our wedding was quite Roman. My hair wasn't parted with a spear, but I did wear a saffron yellow veil and a garland of flowers I picked myself. We had a procession with music and nuts, and the songs were not too rude. My father carried me over the threshold to where Gaius was waiting and I said, 'Ubi tu Gaius, ego Gaia' – 'Where you are, Gaius, there will I be, Gaia'. At first I thought this was a strange thing to say but now I think I know what it means: 'I am your other half, and wherever you are, I will be there, too.'

My wedding was wonderful and exciting and yes, a little frightening, and I'm glad it's over. Now I can settle down in my little house and my own garden and begin to raise a family.

FIVE FRIGHTENING THINGS A ROMAN BRIDE MUST DO

1. She must often agree to marry when she is as young as twelve
2. She must allow her hair to be parted into seven portions with the point of a sharp spear
3. She must submit to hearing crude jokes and lewd songs as she proceeds to the home of the groom
4. She must be dragged from the arms of her mother, or a close female relative, and carried bodily over the threshold so that her foot does not knock it, a bad omen
5. Her long white tunic is belted with a complicated knot that her husband must untie that night

PULCHRA

FULL NAME: Polla Felicia (nicknamed 'Pulchra' which means 'beautiful')

BIRTHDAY: 31 July AD 68

BIRTHPLACE: Neapolis

EYE COLOUR: Blue

HAIR COLOUR: Honey-blonde

FAVOURITE FOOD: Lemon cakes

FAVOURITE PLACE: The Villa Limona, my family's opulent seaside villa

FAVOURITE TIME OF DAY: Early afternoon, being pampered in the baths

TOPICS ASSIGNED BY FLAVIA: Beauty, Roman Society

FASHION AND BEAUTY

I love being beautiful. Pater says it is a privilege and that I must be gracious to people who are not as fortunate. Our cognomen Felix – or Felicia in my case – means 'lucky' or 'fortunate' and I am so fortunate. I am rich, beautiful, intelligent, creative and musical. I can speak Greek as fluently as I speak Latin. That's because pater's family originally come from Greece. Pater writes poetry and plays the lyre. So do I. Mater used to be a patroness of the arts and myriads of poets used to visit us. Some of them still do. I hope to be a patroness and a poetess one day.

But most of all I hope to marry a rich and handsome patrician and live in Rome for part of the year while he attends the Senate. I would so like to visit Rome. Pater and mater have told me all about it. You are so lucky you live near Rome, Flavia. If I lived so close, I would go to poetry readings and dinner parties, to the chariot races and the theatre. Of course I would only watch the higher forms of drama, like tragedy and pantomime. Comedy and mime are so plebeian!

I just know that one day I will meet the right man. He will be just like pater – only younger of course – and he will buy me silks and jewels and a litter with four Ethiopian bearers. Oh, I simply can't wait!

PULCHRA'S TOP FIVE TIPS FOR GETTING A HIGHBORN HUSBAND

1. Live in Rome, where most young patrician men are to be found
2. Have a powerful and influential father (or patron) with lots of connections
3. Go to parties, the theatre and especially the races, to be seen as much as possible
4. Do not let passion cloud your judgement; marry for money and position
5. Always be as beautiful and well-groomed as possible, but also modest and soft-spoken

PULCHRA'S TOP TEN TIPS FOR STAYING BEAUTIFUL

Remember, dearest Flavia, even if you can't be beautiful, you can always be well-groomed!

1. Every Roman girl would like pale skin like mine. The best way to keep your skin fair is to stay out of the sun or use a parasol. Tanned skin will make you look like a field slave! Some ladies use powdered lead to whiten the complexion. It is very silky and nice, but quite expensive.

2. To bleach and soften the skin, I used a special lemon-scented cream. It is made of lard and white tin oxide – whatever that is – and it is scented with lemon oil.

3. To give a natural blush to your cheeks, take a wine-cup with some dried wine in the bottom. Rub your finger gently in the powdered dregs, then brush lightly across your cheekbone. You can also use ochre, grind a little on your make-up palette and brush on cheeks. Use redcurrant juice to stain your lips an attractive pink.

4. To emphasise the eyes, use a little kohl. Kohl is a charcoal grey powder from far-away lands. On your make-up palette, mix the kohl with a little water and use a tiny brush to outline your eyes. Then smudge gently for a natural look.

5. For luminous eyes, brush some powdered shimmering blue stibium across the upper lid of your eye. Be careful! The skin is very delicate here.

6. This year, red hair is quite fashionable. You can buy good quality wigs in Rome, but they are harder to find in the provinces. If you have a red-haired slave-girl, make her cut her hair and have your own wig made from it. To tint your hair red, dye it with a mixture of henna and red wine. To lighten dark hair, use a mixture of vinegar and lye. Of course, if the gods have blessed you with golden hair like mine, don't tamper with it!

7. Use pumice to smooth the rough skin on your heels. The best time is at the baths, between the massage and hairdresser. Pumice is a kind of light porous rock found near volcanoes. We have lots of it here in Surrentum.

8. You can also use pumice to keep your legs smooth and hair-free. Rub the pumice-stone briskly over your legs while your skin is dry. Some people suggest smearing your legs with a mixture of boar's blood and turpentine as a depilatory but I find the smell quite revolting.

9. After your bath, when you've scraped off the oily dead skin, towel yourself briskly and re-apply a lightly scented oil to your face and body. Your skin will look dewy fresh and you'll smell nice, too.

10. To brighten teeth, some people use their own urine as a mouthwash. I think this is positively repulsive. However, I do use a tooth-stick to keep my teeth and gums clean. And I chew mastic gum to keep my mouth kissable and my breath fresh!

And Flavia, dear, do try to avoid undignified
catfights with your friends!

ROMAN SOCIETY

I have told you how to get a husband of the highest social class, so I'm delighted that you asked me to write about Roman society.

They used to call Rome a 'republic', but of course it was really an aristocracy. And it still is. I'm sure you know that.

It helps me to think of Roman society as a pyramid. At the very top is the Emperor. Below him are the aristocrats: men of the patrician class (who must have property worth over 800,000 sesterces) and men like our fathers, who are of the equestrian class. They must have at least 400,000 sesterces to hand. (That used to be the amount necessary for keeping a horse because in the old days every man of the equestrian class had to have his own horse.) We aristocrats are superior to the other classes not just in wealth, but in breeding, intelligence, talent, morals and looks. Just look around you. You can tell an aristocrat immediately. He is tall and walks proudly. He has noble features and he dresses with style.

Then look at the plebeians. They are usually short, with bandy legs and swarthy skin. They scuttle along with subservience draped over them like a cloak. These plebeians – or lower classes – form the bulk of the pyramid. There is a terribly wide gulf between the aristocracy and the plebs. We aristocrats are almost always wealthy, most plebs are desperately poor. But at least they are free Roman citizens.

Beneath the plebs are freedmen, men who used to be slaves but are now free. Some have become extremely wealthy. Do not consider marrying a freedman, Flavia. Not even a rich one. They do not have the quality of a proper aristocrat and the upper classes secretly despise them.

The base of the pyramid is formed by slaves. Don't even think about marrying a slave. That would be too horrid for words. Mater told me about a rich matron who fell in love with a gladiator – a slave! – and ran away with him. The humiliation! The disgrace! The horror!

Girls like you and I have only two choices: patrician or equestrian. And of those two, you should set your sights on a patrician. Why a patrician, if both classes are rich and respected? Well, patricians are better because they can become senators and gain power. Not as much power as they had during the old republic, but still: power. And as any Roman knows: power equals wealth and wealth equals happiness. It's as simple as that!

By the way, there are quite a few old and respected families of the patrician class. If you can marry a man from one of these clans you have done very well. A man with the nomen Aemilius, Claudius, Cornelius, Fabius, Julius, Papirius, Postumius, Quinctius, Servilius or Valerius should do very nicely. (But make sure that he really is a patrician and not one of their freedmen!) You can spot patricians from a distance by the two thick red vertical stripes on their tunics.

Good luck, Flavia! Happy hunting!

NUBIA

REAL NAME: Shepenwepet of the Leopard Clan

BIRTHDAY: 18 August AD 68

ELEMENT: Fire

BIRTHPLACE: Nubia (a desert country south of Egypt)

EYE-COLOUR: Golden brown

FAVOURITE FOOD: Dates

FAVOURITE PLACE: Flavia's inner garden; it is safe and green there

FAVOURITE TIME OF DAY: Night, when the stars are overhead

TOPICS ASSIGNED BY FLAVIA: Freeborn and Slave

Here is about my life, Flavia. It was hard to write but now I finish it I am feeling better a little, and I am happy that you put it in your book for people to know what happens to me. (Please excuse my Latin is still not so good as you and Jonathan and Lupus.)

The night before slave-traders come is warm and velvet. The stars blaze so beauty that it makes my heart hurt. My family and I sit on soft sand around fire. Eldest brother Taharqo plays his flute. He plays Song of the Maiden and Song of the Lost Kid. Our goats are nearby. I hear their bells clanking soft and I smell their odour, mix with smell of burning sandalwood and palm leaves. Our camels are also close by. I hear them chewing their cuds.

I lie on my back with my knees up in front of fire, so that my face is being in shadow. Song of the Lost Kid is making me weep and I do not want others to see. I am thinking how frightened little goat must be who has lost his mother. My dog Nipur comes over to me, as he always does when I am sad. But I am not really sad. I am glad. Glad to be safe with my family and goats and camels.

I move so that I can see mother. She sits rocking littlest sister Seyala in embroidered sling from shoulder to hip. Mother has eyes closed, and in the firelight and starlight it seems her cheeks are wet.

Even my twin brothers Shabaqo and Shebitqo are quiet, and not rolling in the dust as usually.

I look at father and see he was gazing into fire with eyes almost as gold as flames. They are always telling me I have his eyes. When last note of Taharqo's song is carried away on the night breeze, Father begins to tell story.

He tells the story of The Traveller, a young man who travels the world looking for happiness. He travels to the Land of Green, where everything is lush and green like a park, and people live in trees. He travels to the Land of Blue, where everything is water and fish and sky, and people live in a box that floats on the water. He travels to the Land of Red, where everything is made of brick and tile and people do not move from one place to another but stay in one house. He travels to the Land of White, where everything is snow and ice and frost, and people dress in white animal fur. Finally he returns to the Land of Gold, where the sun and sand and goats are golden, and he finds happiness at last with his own family.

That is the last night my family and I spend together. The next night my father and Shebitqo are dead. Nipur and other dogs, too. Goats and camels are being taken as prize. Mother and baby Seyala and I are chained with others from our clan, and with some not from our clan.

We are marched for a very long way. I do not remember those days and nights very well, I am so full of misery. My feet are blister and my throat dry. On that journey many die and are left beside the road for jackals and vultures. My mother and baby sister are among them. I cry and scream and try to stay with them, but the chain is still around my neck and they force me walking on.

Soon I have no more tears. We arrive at Alexandria. For first time, I see the Land of Blue, where everything is water and fish and sky, and some people live in boxes which float on the water. I know

now that these are called ships.

One of the girls is not wanting to go across the board which leads from the land to ship. That is when horrible man called Venalicius throws her in water. She drowns before our eyes while men around us laughed.

You would think that losing everything I do not want to live, but now I am wanting to live more than ever.

FREEBORN AND SLAVE

In the Land of Gold where I come from, there are no slaves. Everyone is free. Many are poor, but as long as we have family and food, music and storytelling, we are content. But then one day slave-traders come. They are killing my father and the strong men of our clan and they are enslaving the women and children.

Then they bring me to your town, Flavia, to Ostia – the Land of Red. Now I see many slaves. They do not all have dark skin like me. Some have olive skin, or white, or brown. Many are from countries Romans have captured. If a town resists Roman rule, then soldiers go in and kill all men and all boys of warrior age. Then they take women and children back to Rome to sell for slaves. Many slaves in Rome are now Jews, for the Romans destroyed their great city Jerusalem ten years ago, and were enslaving many people who lived there.

Sometimes kidnappers steal freeborn children to sell into slavery. This is not the law, but if they are taking you somewhere far away then how will your parents find you?

You can become a slave in other ways than being captured. If you are born to slave parents then you are a 'homegrown' slave, a verna.

Even some freeborn families are so poor that they must sell their own children into slavery. I think of that poor man who was owing so much money that he had to sell himself to pay his debts. Now he works as slave in bakery here in Ostia.

Aristo was telling me that one clever Roman senator suggests making all slaves wear some special clothing or brand or collar, so that citizens could tell who was slave and who was free. But then another senator shows that if slaves see they are many, they might be revolting against their masters!

Revolt is not good. If one slave kills his master, all slaves in that household must die. And if slave is running away, he can be punished by crucifixion. That is when they are nailing you alive to a cross. It is taking you three days to die.

Felix entertains the four detectives in his
dining room, attended by slaves

Some masters do not crucify runaway slave. Instead, they brand the slave with a warning. Another slave at bakery has words 'tene me' branded across his forehead. This means 'hold me'. He is not trying to run away any more.

Many slaves are treated well and are happy, especially house-slaves. I think your Alma is happy and also your door-slave Caudex.

Sometimes slaves are being set free. If over thirty years old, they can become Roman citizens. When a slave is freed, he takes his master's first two names. If your father set Caudex free, he would become Marcus Flavius Caudex. He would now be Roman citizen and any children he would have would be freeborn Roman citizens. I think this is one good thing about the Romans. If you work hard to gain your freedom and achieve great things, they don't mind that you used to be a slave.

You were very kind to me, Flavia. You were never treating me bad and after only a few months you invited me to recline beside you to set me free. I was afraid to say yes at first. Where would I go? How would I live? Then you were saying I can still live with you. I was happy and say yes.

Scraius of Stabia demonstrates what happens to runaway slaves: crucifixion

PLINY THE YOUNGER

FULL NAME: Gaius Plinius Caecilius Secundus

BIRTHDAY: AD 61

BIRTHPLACE: Novum Comum (near modern Lake Como)

CLASS: Equestrian, but with hopes of becoming Patrician

MILITARY SERVICE: Soon to serve with the Syrian legion

FAVOURITE PLACE: Anywhere shady and quiet, where I can read or write

FAVOURITE TIME OF DAY: In bed before sleep, going over the events of the day

TOPIC ASSIGNED BY FLAVIA: The Eruption of Vesuvius

THE ERUPTION OF VESUVIUS

You ask me for an account of my activities on that terrible day, dear Flavia. Although my mind shrinks from remembering, I will tell you, for you told me of my uncle's death – and of your own suffering – and that must not have been easy, either. So let me plunge right in and begin.

My mother and I were staying with her brother – my uncle – Gaius Plinius Secundus. He had recently been appointed admiral of the fleet by his friend the emperor Vespasian, and was on active duty in Misenum, on the Bay of Naples. I was seventeen at the time, but have since celebrated my eighteenth birthday.

We had spent the morning reading, me in the cool shade of a colonnade – for it was a hot, heavy day – my uncle in the sun, as was his habit. When it began to get too hot for him, he took a cold bath and a light lunch and resumed his studies in the shade near me.

My mother was the first to notice the strange cloud rising across the bay. It looked like a giant grey umbrella pine and must have been five miles high. We ran to an upper room and stared open-mouthed, astounded. Because of the distance and haze, we didn't realise the cloud was rising from the green cone of Vesuvius. We didn't know until afterwards that it was a volcanic eruption.

Being a natural historian, my uncle wanted to investigate the enormous cloud. He invited me to come, but I was busy finishing some essays for him on Livy and decided to remain behind. I wish now that I had gone with him. Perhaps if I had, he might still be alive. That was the last time my mother and I saw him alive.

He met a messenger on the way to the docks and this messenger convinced him to go to rescue our friend Rectina, who had a villa in Herculaneum, at the foot of Vesuvius. However, my uncle was unable to reach her, so instead he made for Stabia, four miles south. As you well know, that was where he met his end.

For my uncle had a weak chest and was somewhat asthmatic. The ash fall and sulphur fumes did not harm those of you with a stronger constitution but for him it was fatal. Thanks to your eyewitness account, I know he died bravely and with fortitude.

After my uncle left us, I continued to read my books, then bathed and dined with my mother, despite the continuing earthquakes and strange brown colour of the sky. We retired uneasily to our respective bedrooms, but the trembling of the earth became more and more violent and I could only doze. Finally, a particularly violent tremor shook me out of bed. I slipped on my tunic and started for the door, intending to check on my mother. At that moment she rushed into my room, equally concerned about me.

The columns and walls were swaying around us, so we agreed to go outside and sit for a while in the open space before the house. I tried to keep my mind calm by continuing my studies of Livy. Presently a friend arrived and asked us what in Hades we were doing sitting there during such a disaster. But what could we do? Panic? I continued to read by the light of an oil-lamp.

However, by dawn the buildings were tottering so violently that we decided to join the fleeing crowds.

At first we thought to go by carriage but a terrifying thing happened. When our carriages were brought, they seemed to be alive, moving back and forth in different directions, even though the ground there was level. Unsettled by this portent, we decided to continue on foot. As we went along the coastal road, I saw that the sea had been sucked back, leaving the poor sea creatures exposed on dry land, as it were.

Suddenly screams made us turn and we saw another dreadful sight. A huge cloud – as black as octopus ink – rushing towards us. I grasped my mother's hand and we ran in panic but the cloud soon engulfed us in a terrible darkness. It was not the darkness of night, but that of a windowless room when the lamp has been extinguished. Many people thought they were dying and even grown men called for their mothers.

Some people prayed to the gods, others cursed them. I remained silent; if the whole world was perishing, what use would screaming be?

My mother and I remained huddled together in terrified silence, not daring to move lest a false step send us into a ditch or over some unseen precipice.

Presently it became a little lighter. But it was the lurid light of flames, not of the sun, and with it came a new fear: that of being overwhelmed by a cloud of flames and burned alive. Thankfully, the flames did not come any closer and soon it grew dark again as billows of black ash began to pour from the sky. I now know the ash had been falling elsewhere until now, but a westerly shift in the wind drove it towards us.

Now a new danger presented itself. We had to stand every half hour or so and shake off the thickly falling ash, or else we would have been buried alive by it, even crushed by its weight.

At last, after what seemed like days, the light returned. It was daylight, but like no day I have ever seen. The sun was sick and pale, as if during an eclipse. We returned to my uncle's house. To our great dismay we discovered that he had not returned, and we saw everything covered with terrible drifts of ash.

We tried to sleep that night, but the earth was still suffering violent tremors and we had frequent visits by neighbours hysterical with fear. Some urged us to leave, but how could we until we had learned the fate of my poor uncle?

> *Literature is both a joy and my comfort to me. There is no happiness it cannot increase and no sorrow it cannot console.*
> Pliny the Younger *(Letter 19.1)*

TITUS

FULL NAME: Imperator Titus Caesar Vespasianus Augustus

BIRTH NAME: Titus Flavius Vespasianus

BIRTHDAY: 30 December AD 39

BIRTHPLACE: Rome

MILITARY SERVICE: In Germania, Britannia and Judaea

FAVOURITE TIME OF DAY: End of the day when my duties are completed, sitting with a companion in a breeze-cooled upper room of my palace on the Palatine Hill

INFORMATION RESPECTFULLY REQUESTED BY FLAVIA: Emperors of Rome

EMPERORS OF ROME

He was very handsome, with a great deal of natural authority and grace. He was exceptionally strong, though short and somewhat stocky. He had a remarkable memory, and a gift for the arts of both war and peace: he was skilful in arms and horsemanship, but could write and speak eloquently Greek as well as Latin. He was also musical, and could both sing and play most agreeably . . . in addition, he could imitate any handwriting and used to brag that he could have been the best of forgers.

Suetonius *(Titus 1.3 passim)*

Your request that I write a few words on the emperors of Rome is a timely one. I was just compiling such a history for my daughter Julia. I will ask my scribe to copy it out and send it to you, rough though it is.

One hundred and twenty-three years ago, Julius Caesar made himself dictator

for life. Within a month he was dead, assassinated by outraged senators who feared he would gain complete power. Caesar's nephew Octavian did not make the same mistake. He realised that Rome was ripe for a sole ruler, but instead of calling himself 'king' or 'dictator', he became consul, a magistracy elected every year. That way, he did not seem to desire unlimited, permanent power. But of course he did. And he continued to hold this position – and a good many other powerful positions – year after year.

Of course, intelligent Romans knew exactly what he was up to, but they were so exhausted by years of civil war and so sickened by the shedding of blood, that they welcomed a firm, fair hand on the tiller of the state.

At one point, the Senate wanted to address Octavian by a special name. At first he wanted to be called 'Romulus', but when he realised this made it seem as if he wanted to be king, he allowed the Senate to bestow the title 'Augustus' or 'Majestic' on him instead. He received the name Gaius Julius Caesar in his grand-uncle's will, along with adoptive sonship and all that man's riches. Octavian called himself 'Imperator', which as you know means 'Commander' or 'General' and does not have the bad associations of a word like 'King' or 'Tyrant'. And later, after Julius Caesar was proclaimed divine, he called himself Imperator Caesar divi filius Augustus: 'General Caesar, son of the deified one, Majestic'. Ever since, most emperors have taken either the name Caesar or Augustus, or both.

My father Vespasian was first Imperator Titus Flavius Vespasianus Caesar, and later Imperator Caesar Vespasianus Augustus. I became Titus Caesar Vespasianus in the summer of his accession. By that time the appellation 'Caesar' had come to mean something like 'crown prince'. Only after the death of my father, did I received the title 'Augustus', the true mark of a ruling emperor.

The Romans hate the term 'monarchy' so much that they will not call their rulers dictators or kings or anything similar . . . so the emperors have taken . . . the functions – titles included – which were popular under the republic . . . for example, they frequently become consuls, and they often hold the title proconsul and they hold the title imperator for life . . .

Dio Cassius *(Roman History 53.17.2-5)*

Pulchra to her dear Flavia: One of pater's friends has a son who is our age. He wants to be a biographer when he is older. He has been doing assignments for his tutor on the first ten emperors of Rome. Pater asked his friend's son to send me some of the most exciting facts he has compiled and I just received it. I am forwarding it on to you, and I do hope it's in time for your book. The son's name is Gaius Suetonius Tranquillus. Perhaps we will meet him some day.

INTERESTING FACTS ABOUT THE FIRST TEN EMPERORS OF ROME

BY GAIUS SUETONIUS TRANQUILLUS

1. AUGUSTUS

(also known as Gaius Octavian or Augustus Caesar)

Became emperor just over one hundred years ago. He bragged that he 'found Rome brick and left her marble'. He also had a month named after him. Everyone agrees his rule was a golden age. He had the son of Caesar and Cleopatra murdered, but spared her children by Antonius.

2. TIBERIUS

(born Tiberius Claudius Nero, then Imperator Tiberius Caesar Augustus)

It is rumoured that his mother Livia by poisoning her husband Augustus as soon as he named Tiberius his heir. Admiral Pliny once called him 'the gloomiest of men'.

3. CALIGULA

(also known as Gaius Caesar Augustus Germanicus)

Great grandson of Augustus. His nickname 'Caligula' means 'baby-boots', because as a child he went on campaign with his father Germanicus and wore small soldiers' boots. By all accounts he was a cruel man and was assassinated by his own Praetorian Guard.

4. CLAUDIUS

(born Tiberius Claudius Drusus, then Tiberius Claudius Caesar Augustus Germanicus)

He was the uncle of Caligula. He had a

speech impediment and occasionally suffered fits, but despite these handicaps was a good emperor. Among his many achievements were the conquest of Britannia and the building of a new harbour at Ostia. He loved gambling so much that he wrote a book on dice. He died suddenly. Many suspect that he was poisoned by his fourth wife (also his niece) Agrippina, so that her son Nero would become Emperor. Claudius's son Britannicus was poisoned, too.

5. NERO

(born Lucius Domitius Ahenobarbus, then Nero Claudius Caesar Augustus Germanicus)

Grand-nephew and adopted son of Claudius, and son of Agrippina. He would rather have been an actor or chariot driver than emperor. After one of the worst fires in Rome's history he built his Golden House on the ruins. He also executed many noble men whom he accused of conspiring against him. Finally he committed suicide at the age of thirty. Some people say he faked his death and recently others claim to have seen him in Parthia!

6. GALBA

(Servius Sulpicius Galba, then Servius Galba Imperator Caesar Augustus)

The Pythian oracle warned Nero to 'beware the age of 68'. Nero thought this referred to the age he would be when he died, but it turned out to be Galba's age when he succeeded Nero. Galba was the first emperor in the so-called 'year of the four emperors'. He only ruled for seven months and a week before being assassinated.

7. OTHO

(born Marcus Salvius Otho, then Imperator Marcus Otho Caesar Augustus)

Of Etruscan descent, Otho only ruled for three months before he was assassinated. Earlier in his life, his wife Poppaea left him to become Nero's mistress.

8. VITELLIUS

(born Aulus Vitellius, then Aulus Vitellius Germanicus Imperator Augustus)

He ruled for less than a year before being struck down by assassins and thrown into the Tiber.

9. VESPASIAN

(born Titus Flavius Sabinus Vespasianus, then Imperator Caesar Vespasianus Augustus)

The so-called 'Mule-driver' was born in the Sabine Hills. He was a bull-necked soldier who served in Germania and Britannia, among other places. He was serving in Judaea, to quell the Jewish revolt, when he heard he had been proclaimed Emperor and hurried back to Rome, leaving his son Titus in command. The first of the Flavian dynasty, he ruled for ten years and is known for building the great Flavian amphitheatre from the spoils of conquered Jerusalem.

10. TITUS

(born Titus Flavius Vespasianus, then Imperator Titus Caesar Vespasianus Augustus)

Before he became emperor, he lived a riotous life and did not escape public criticism: everyone thought he would be a 'second Nero'. He had a notorious passion for a Jewish queen named Berenice, but when he became emperor he sent her away. Since then, he has shown himself to be a kind and fair emperor. However, the first year of his reign has already been blighted by three terrible disasters: the eruption of Vesuvius in Campania, a terrible plague in Rome and a fire in that same city that lasted three days and three nights.

LUPUS

FULL OR REAL NAME: Lukos of Symi

BIRTHDAY: 15 February AD 71

HIS ELEMENT: Water

BIRTHPLACE: Symi, a Greek island of sponge-divers

EYE-COLOUR: Sea green

FAVOURITE FOOD: Oysters, because they slip down easily

FAVOURITE PLACE: Swimming in the sea or splashing in the baths

FAVOURITE TIME OF DAY: Midday, when the sea is warmest

TOPICS ASSIGNED BY FLAVIA: Roman Art, Writing

I WAS BORN ON THE ISLAND OF SYMI. MY FATHER AND GRANDFATHER AND ALMOST EVERY OTHER MAN ON THE ISLAND WERE SPONGE-DIVERS. MOST WERE TOO POOR EVEN TO BE ABLE TO AFFORD THE SPONGES THEY RISKED THEIR LIVES FOR. BUT WE WERE HAPPY. WE HAD THE SUN AND THE SEA AND GRILLED FISH AND LAUGHTER. I LEARNED TO SWIM BEFORE I LEARNED TO WALK.

WHEN I WAS SIX YEARS OLD, A TERRIBLE THING HAPPENED, AS YOU KNOW. I ENDED UP IN OSTIA, VERY FAR FROM SYMI. AFTER THAT TERRIBLE THING, I DID NOT TRUST ANYONE. ANGER SNARLED INSIDE ME LIKE A WILD DOG OR A WOLF. LIKE AN ANIMAL, I MADE MY HOME IN THE TOMBS OUTSIDE OSTIA.

SOMETIMES I BEGGED. SOMETIMES I STOLE. WHEN IT GOT COLD I SLEPT NEAR THE FURNACE OF THE BATHS, WHERE IT WAS WARM.

THEN YOU FOUND ME WHEN I FELL OUT OF THE TREE. DO YOU REMEMBER? I LIKED IT THAT YOU ASKED ME TO HELP FIND THE PERSON WHO KILLED JONATHAN'S DOG. AFTER A WHILE I LEARNED TO TRUST YOU A LITTLE.

IT WAS GOOD THAT ARISTO HAS TAUGHT ME TO WRITE. NOW I CAN SPEAK WITH A WAX TABLET. IT MAKES MY HAND ACHE SOMETIMES, BUT IT'S BETTER THAN HAVING TO ACT OUT EVERYTHING.

I LIKE DRAWING AND I LIKE SPYING ON PEOPLE. I AM HAPPY THAT YOU OFTEN ASK ME TO HELP YOU SOLVE MYSTERIES. I LIKE IT WHEN YOU ASK ME TO DRAW A PICTURE OF THE CULPRIT OR THE PERSON WE ARE SEARCHING FOR. I LIKE IT THAT YOU ALWAYS ASK ME TO SPY ON PEOPLE. I LIKE IT WHEN YOU ASK ME TO PUT ON A DISGUISE. I THINK THE FOUR OF US ARE A GOOD TEAM. WE USUALLY CATCH THE CULPRIT.

I AM NOT SO ANGRY INSIDE ANY MORE. BUT SOMETIMES WHEN I

REMEMBER WHAT HAPPENED, OR IF SOMEONE IS MEAN TO ME, THE ANGER INSIDE ME SNARLS LIKE A DOG. WHEN IT DOES YOU HAD BETTER WATCH OUT!

ART

I HAVE ALWAYS BEEN GOOD AT DRAWING.

EVEN BEFORE I COULD READ AND WRITE I COULD DRAW. I CAN LOOK AT A FACE AND THEN DRAW IT PERFECTLY. I'M NOT BRAGGING. IT'S THE TRUTH.

I CAN ALSO PAINT A GOOD PORTRAIT IN ENCAUSTIC. A PORTRAIT IS A PICTURE OF A PERSON. ENCAUSTIC IS COLOURED WAX. IT'S TRICKY TO USE BUT I WATCHED SOME PAINTERS ONE TIME AND QUICKLY GOT THE HANG OF IT. YOU HAVE TO WORK WHILE THE WAX IS WARM. NOT HOT. NOT COLD. BUT WARM.

I ALSO LEARNED HOW TO PAINT FRESCOS BY WATCHING. A FRESCO IS A PAINTING IN FRESH PLASTER. YOU HAVE TO APPLY THE PAINT WHILE THE PLASTER IS STILL DAMP. THAT WAY THE PLASTER SUCKS UP THE COLOUR AND WHEN IT DRIES THE PAINT IS PART OF THE WALL. LAST DECEMBER A FRESCO PAINTER WAS PUTTING A FRESCO OF THE TWELVE TASKS OF HERCULES ON FLAVIA'S DINING ROOM WALL. I WATCHED HIM CAREFULLY. AS HE WAS FINISHING THE LAST PANEL HE SUDDENLY COLLAPSED WITH A FEVER. THE PLASTER WAS STILL DAMP. CAUDEX CARRIED HIM TO DOCTOR MORDECAI NEXT DOOR. IT WAS UP TO ME TO FINISH THE PANEL BEFORE THE PLASTER DRIED. SO I DID. IT WAS EXCELLENT. I'M NOT BRAGGING. IT'S THE TRUTH.

MOSAICS ARE PICTURES DONE WITH THOUSANDS OF TINY TESSERAE (SQUARES) OF MARBLE, STONE, EVEN GLASS. I WOULD NEVER HAVE THE PATIENCE TO DO A MOSAIC. THEY TAKE DAYS AND DAYS. BUT I

LIKE LOOKING AT THEM BECAUSE THEY OFTEN SHOW SCENES FROM GREEK MYTHOLOGY. I LIKE GREEK MYTHOLOGY FOR TWO REASONS. ONE, I AM GREEK. TWO, MANY MYTHS ARE VERY GORY AND BLOODY AND I LIKE THAT.

I PROBABLY WOULDN'T BE A SCULPTOR EITHER. IT WOULD TAKE TOO MUCH TIME TO CHIP AWAY ALL THAT MARBLE. I LIKE TO WORK FAST.

I LIKE APPLYING ENCAUSTIC PAINT BEFORE IT GETS COOL, OR FINISHING A FRESCO BEFORE THE WALL DRIES. THAT'S WHAT I LIKE DOING.

WRITING

WHEN I FIRST CAME TO ITALIA I COULDN'T WRITE. NOT BECAUSE I WAS STUPID, BUT BECAUSE NOBODY

HAD EVER TAUGHT ME. MY FATHER WAS A SPONGE-DIVER AND MY MOTHER WOVE AND COOKED. THEY DIDN'T HAVE TO KNOW HOW TO READ OR WRITE. NOBODY ON OUR ISLAND DID.

BUT WHEN I MET JONATHAN AND FLAVIA AND NUBIA, THEY INVITED ME TO ATTEND LESSONS WITH THEM. ARISTO SAYS I LEARNED FASTER THAN ANYONE HE'S EVER MET. SOMETIMES HIS LESSONS ARE BORING BUT MOSTLY THEY ARE GOOD. HE SAYS HE MAKES HIS LESSONS INTERESTING BY USING THE TASTY BAIT OF FUN OR REVOLTING FACTS TO CAPTURE OUR ATTENTION. WE ARE HIS FISHES AND HE IS THE FISHERMAN.

REASON I LEARNED TO WRITE SO QUICKLY IS NOT BECAUSE ARISTO IS A GOOD TEACHER. IT IS BECAUSE I

INSIDE OF EACH LEAF IS COATED WITH YELLOW BEESWAX. I USE A SHARP BRONZE INSTRUMENT CALLED A STYLUS TO SCRATCH LETTERS IN THE SOFT WAX. THEN I USE THE FLAT END OF THE STYLUS TO SMOOTH THE WAX AGAIN AND ERASE WHAT I'VE WRITTEN. YOU CAN ALSO GET WAX TABLETS WITH RED OR BLACK WAX. RED WAX IS COLOURED WITH CINNABAR AND BLACK WITH SOOT. I HAVE TWO SPARE WAX TABLETS.

I SOMETIMES WRITE ON PAPYRUS WITH A QUILL PEN AND BLACK INK. PAPYRUS IS MADE OF AN EGYPTIAN WATER PLANT. IT'S CUT AND POUNDED AND PRESSED AND DRIED. IT MAKES YELLOW TEXTURED SHEETS THAT YOU CAN WRITE ON. THAT'S WHAT THEY MAKE SCROLLS FROM. IT'S QUITE TRICKY TO WRITE ON BECAUSE THE PEN CAN JUMP A LITTLE ON THE TEXTURED SURFACE AND MAKE A BLOB OF INK.

AM VERY CLEVER AND DETERMINED. I'M NOT BRAGGING. IT'S THE TRUTH.

MY FAVOURITE THING TO WRITE ON IS MY WAX TABLET. IT HAS TWO LEAVES OF WOOD HINGED AT ONE SIDE WITH SOME STRING. SOME PEOPLE CALL IT A 'DIPTYCH'. THE

ONCE I TRIED WRITING ON A SCRAP OF PARCHMENT. PARCHMENT IS

TREATED ANIMAL SKIN. IT'S SMOOTHED WITH PUMICE AND THEN DUSTED WITH CHALK AND THE PEN FLOWS SO SMOOTHLY ACROSS THE SURFACE THAT YOU NEVER MAKE A BLOB. BUT IT'S VERY EXPENSIVE AND ONLY USED FOR IMPORTANT DOCUMENTS, LIKE IMPERIAL DECREES.

SOME PEOPLE EVEN WRITE ON SMALL WAFER-THIN SCRAPS OF WOOD. I TRIED THAT ONCE AND JONATHAN'S DOG TIGRIS ATE IT. I THINK HE THOUGHT IT WAS A DOG BISCUIT.

ONE OF MY FAVOURITE METHODS OF WRITING IS ON WALLS. YOU CAN USE PAINT OR CHARCOAL OR JUST SCRATCH LETTERS INTO THE WALL. IT'S CALLED GRAFFITI. THE ROMANS LOVE GRAFFITI. SOME GRAFFITI IS FOR IMPORTANT PUBLIC ANNOUNCEMENTS OR ELECTIONS. BUT MY FAVOURITE GRAFFITI IS PERSONAL, FUNNY AND RUDE GRAFFITI, LIKE 'DON'T PEE HERE; THERE ARE STINGING NETTLES' OR 'CRESCENS THE RETIARIUS NETS MEN BY DAY AND GIRLS BY NIGHT!'

LUPUS'S TOP FIVE TIPS FOR SPYING ON PEOPLE

1. IT HELPS IF YOU ARE SMALL AND CAN HIDE IN UNLIKELY PLACES

2. WEAR SILENT-SOLED SHOES OR BOOTS FOR FOLLOWING PEOPLE; SANDALS SLAP ON THE GROUND WHEN YOU RUN

3. HIDE RIGHT OUT IN THE OPEN SOMETIMES (I PRETEND TO BE A BEGGAR AND NOBODY NOTICES ME)

4. THE BATHS ARE USEFUL FOR EAVESDROPPING (PEOPLE TELL ALL KINDS OF SECRETS WHEN THEY ARE NAKED)

5. BE PATIENT (THE SUSPECT USUALLY APPEARS WHEN YOU ARE JUST ABOUT TO GIVE UP AND GO HOME)

PLINY THE ELDER

FULL NAME: Gaius Plinius Secundus

BIRTHDAY: AD 24

BIRTHPLACE: Comum (modern Lake Como)

CLASS: Equestrian

MILITARY SERVICE: With Titus in Germania

APPOINTMENTS: Admiral of the fleet at Misenum

FAVOURITE PLACE: Lying in the sun on a summer's day, listening to a slave reading

FAVOURITE TIME OF DAY: Morning, when I am fresh and alert

TOPIC ASSIGNED BY FLAVIA: Scholarship

Flavia's note: I asked Pliny's friend Tascius to tell me his recolletions of Admiral Pliny as a scholar. Here is what he wrote.

SCHOLARSHIP

by Titus Tascius Pomponianus

My dear Flavia. It is so good to hear from you, all the more so as you have asked me for my recollections of Admiral Pliny. This has made me think fondly of a dear friend, now sadly departed. You asked me especially to talk about his 'scholarship.' This I shall do with pleasure.

I first met Pliny about twenty years ago, when he came to our seaside villa in Stabia to visit my father. Even then Pliny was a passionate scholar. You rarely saw him without a wax tablet in his hand or without a slave reading from a scroll.

He had an insatiable thirst for knowledge and told me once that he wished he could spend every moment of his life studying the world's riches and its variety of life.

At that time he had only written one other book, a rather juvenile but charming tract on some cavalry skills he had recently acquired. But at the time I met him, he was engaged in writing a biography of my adoptive father, whom he greatly admired. He spent quite a bit of time with us and I got to know him well.

The thing I particularly noticed was his hatred of wasting time. I recall on one occasion, a slave was reading to us at dinner and his pronunciation was sloppy. I asked the slave to re-read the passage.

'Did you not understand it?' asked Pliny.

'Why, yes,' I replied. 'But I want him to learn correct pronunciation.'

'My dear friend,' he chided, 'we have now lost precious minutes when he could have been reading on.'

Such was his passion for making the most of every moment.

I thought it might amuse you to see a list of the books he wrote in his lifetime:

1. *On Throwing a Javelin from Horseback* (one volume) He wrote this while serving in the cavalry in Germania, I believe.

2. *On the Life of Publius Pomponius Secundus* (two volumes) Written as an homage to my adoptive father, who was also his friend.

3. *The German Wars* (twenty volumes) He told me once that Drusus, the brother of the Emperor Tiberius, came to him in a dream and commanded him to write this full account of Rome's wars in Germania.

4. *The Scholar* (three volumes) His excellent and succinct manual on oratory.

5. *Problems in Grammar* (eight volumes) Pliny wrote this during the reign of Nero, when it was fatal to write anything even slightly controversial. He reckoned grammar was a safe subject, and unlikely to offend anyone.

6. *A Continuation of the History of Aufidius Bassus* (thirty-one volumes) Continuation of a history by Bassus, who died before it was completed

7. *A Natural History* (thirty-seven volumes) His opus magnum. If he is remembered for any book, I believe it will be this one. This book best reflected his love of learning and passion for the world.

Gaius Plinius Secundus was a soldier, a lawyer, an admiral and an advisor to the Emperor. But two thousand years from now, I suspect he will be remembered as a scholar.

And I believe that's what he himself would have wanted.

Flavia's note: Poor Admiral Pliny has sadly gone to the shades, never to return. I composed a list of tips for efficiency from what he told me and from what I observed. (A detectrix has to be a good observer.) I've put it down on the next page as if he was writing it himself.

ADMIRAL PLINY'S
TOP FIVE TIPS
FOR MAKING THE MOST OF YOUR TIME

1. When you are riding in your sedan chair, have a slave walk beside you and read from a scroll. That way you won't waste a minute.

2. Apply the same principle when you are sunbathing or having a massage. Have a slave read to you. Keep your wax tablet and notebook close at hand, or a scribe to take notes.

3. Don't recline on a couch to eat. Instead, sit at a table, it's easier to jot down notes while your slave reads to you.

4. Teach yourself to write quickly and using very small letters. That way you can cover more papyrus and in a quicker time.

5. Get up very early before anyone else; that's the best time to work. After such an early start, I often take a short nap after lunch. But when I wake up, start over as if it's a second day! I work after dinner, too, if it's still light.

ALMA

FULL NAME: Alma

BIRTHDAY: Unknown, I think I am about twenty-eight

BIRTHPLACE: Rome

EYE-COLOUR: Hazel

HAIR COLOUR: Brown

FAVOURITE PLACE: In my kitchen, trying out new dishes

FAVOURITE TIME OF DAY: Dinner-time, when I can hear the murmurs of appreciation from the dining room while Caudex and I nibble leftovers in the kitchen.

TOPICS ASSIGNED BY FLAVIA: Food and Drink, Entertainment and Dining, Recipes

MY LIFE SO FAR

(As dictated to Flavia . . .)

I don't believe I have ever told you this, Flavia, but I was found as a baby abandoned among the tombs on the Via Appia outside Rome. A rich family took me in and raised me to be their daughter's personal slave. I was happy enough, until my mistress married. She was not content with her lot, and after a while she began to beat me. She died of a fever aged twenty, without ever bearing any children. (I believe that is why she was unhappy, poor thing, because she was barren.) Her husband soon remarried and as his new wife had her own maid, he sold me in the slave-market. A nice sea captain from Ostia bought me to look after his little girl. The sea captain was your father and the little girl was you! Your mother had recently died in childbirth, and your little twin brothers too, and your father was so very sad. My heart melted for him. You were very sweet, too, though somewhat strong-willed and precocious. Yes, even then! But I could not have loved you more. I'm afraid you know this quite well and as a result you twist me like a skein of wool around your thumb, and get me to agree to all sorts of things I ought not agree to!

Your father installed me in this house on Green Fountain Street in Ostia. I have always liked it here. Ostia is smaller than Rome, of course, but no less interesting to me. Your father was often away and we three slaves enjoyed a certain amount of freedom, as long as we did our chores. I say three, but you will remember that poor Gusto died when a donkey kicked him in the head, so now it is only me and Caudex. I took over Gusto's duties and at the advanced age of 28 – or thereabouts – I finally found my calling. I do so enjoy cooking – and tasting! I also love shopping. I can see my friends and gossip with the stall-holders. I have since become a bit of an expert on food. And I adore cooking for you and your father and your friends. Preparing food is my way of saying I love you.

FOOD AND DRINK

You asked me to talk a little about food here in Ostia. I have only three words: wheat, grapes and olives.

Those are the staple foods of our great Roman empire. Wheat for bread, grapes for wine, and olives for a myriad of uses, not least olive oil. Those are the most important foods, but here are some of the other foods I use.

Ostia is famous for its cabbages, but we also have carrots, turnips, red and white onions, radishes, celery, leeks, mushrooms, beets, sorrel, mallow, truffles, chard, chick peas, broad beans, gourds, squash, broccoli, chives, spinach, lettuce, watercress, chicory, rocket, endive, fennel, artichokes, thistle, asparagus, olives and garlic. We also eat the green 'tops' of butcher's broom, clematis, rue, mallow, wild radish and even some thorn bushes.

Ostia melons are world famous and nearby Laurentum is known for its mulberry trees. But we also have figs, dates, apples, plums, prunes, pears, cherries, pomegranate and quince. More exotic are peaches, apricots and lemons. I have only seen an orange once, and I have never tasted one . . . they are extremely rare.

Considering we live in a seaport, fish is quite expensive and not all that easy to find. But on a good day you might find one or more of the following at the Marina Forum: sole, bass, mackerel, sturgeon, tuna, turbot, red mullet, anchovies, sardines, shark, eels, oysters, clams, lobster, squid and octopus. I never serve octopus when Lupus comes to dinner.

Here on Green Fountain Street, we mainly eat chicken or fish, but I will not turn up my nose at goat or lamb, veal or pork. The children's tutor, Aristo, loves hunting. So does our next-door neighbour, Jonathan ben Mordecai. Between the two of them I often serve rabbit, venison, pigeons, quail, fig-peckers and once a small boar. One dish I have never tried is dormice stuffed with chopped sow's udders. However, I do fancy a snail now and then. Some people say that if you feed them on milk soaked mint you get mint-flavoured snails. Personally I prefer to just fry them up in garlic oil. Then I put them back in their shells and serve them as a tasty gustatio.

The hills just south of here pasture goats, sheep and cattle, so I can easily buy milk, yogurt, cream, soured cream, buttermilk and cheeses of all sorts and descriptions: some as big and round as a wagon-wheel, others soft and creamy and sprinkled with herbs. I do love cheese.

Garum is the Romans' favourite seasoning. This pungent dark liquid made of fermented fish entrails sounds disgusting, but I must confess I have acquired a taste for it.

It's very good on most foods, and you can sweeten it with honey for an exotic sauce. When seasoning food, I also use vinegar, honey, salt, peppercorns, myrtle berries, garlic, basil, oregano, chervil, marjoram, bay leaf, thyme, mint, sage, rue, coriander, caraway seed, mustard seed, chives, cumin, dill, aniseed, fennel, parsley, rose petals, bay leaves, grape leaves, mastic and whatever takes my fancy. Saffron is very popular among the upper classes these days, but it is extemely expensive.

As for drink, your father likes his wine. His favourite used to be the vintage from your uncle's vineyards, but since Vesuvius erupted he'll have to look elsewhere. It is fitting for you children to drink well-watered wine, or

posca. Posca is a refreshing drink made of water with a splash of vinegar. It's the soldiers' favourite tipple. I have also been known to serve grape juice, pomegranate juice, barley water and buttermilk. Peach juice is very refreshing in the summer, but it attracts wasps.

In my own cooking, I use almonds, walnuts, pine nuts, hazelnuts, chestnuts, pistachio nuts, lentils, barley, millet and spelt. And wheat, of course. Egyptian wheat. The granaries here in Ostia are bursting with it. I shop daily at Pistor the baker's. He does the best poppy seed rolls in the Empire. I admit it. I'm partial to Pistor's honey-sesame pastries. Here in Ostia we have many bakeries where you can buy pastries made with wheat, honey, nuts, cheese and dried or candied fruit. Still, I find it easiest to end the meal with fresh or dried fruit. As the saying goes: 'From the egg to the apple'. Nothing like a crunchy red apple to finish off a good meal.

ENTERTAINING AND DINING

The Roman dining room is called a triclinium because it usually has three couches on which diners recline. Romans lie on their left-hand side to leave the right hand free for eating. (As I have told you many times, never use the left hand for eating or passing food, this is considered very rude!)

Up to four people can recline on the couch, lying at an angle with their feet near the wall and their heads towards the tables set before it. They say the perfect number of people for a dinner party is nine – yes, the number of the muses – or three per couch.

Now, if you are facing a dining room, the couch on the left is called the 'lectus imus' or lowest couch, the one in the middle is the middle couch and the one on the right is the 'lectus summus', the highest couch. The host usually reclines at the far end of the left hand couch and the guest of honour next to him at the bottom of the middle couch. That is the place of honour. I need to remember that because I must always serve the guest of honour first.

Children do not normally recline at Roman dinner parties (in fact you should not really attend dinner parties) but sometimes on informal occasions Captain Geminus lets you and your friends climb up onto the couches.

When the guests arrive a slave must take off their sandals, wash and dry their feet, then give them linen dining slippers. Caudex usually does this in the atrium. We usually we give the dinner-guests garlands at the beginning of the meal though some hosts do not give them out until the wine is served at the end. I will never forget the first time Doctor Mordecai came to dinner. He put his garland over his turban and it looked so peculiar!

Guests usually bring their own napkin and sometimes their own spoon and knife, too. Often the host will let them take home some tasty morsels in their napkins. I disapprove of that. It means fewer leftovers for me and Caudex!

Dinner usually begins late in the

afternoon so that guests can make their way home before dark. Ostia is not as dangerous as Rome, but you do not want to be traipsing about, half tipsy and with your napkin full of delicacies! You are just asking to be robbed. Still, if the party is going well and if it's winter, it is often dark by the time our guests leave. The Captain always sends Caudex with a torch, to make sure they get home safely. Luckily that's not a problem for our most frequent guests: Doctor Mordecai and his family live right next door!

I recently found this invitation that you wrote, inviting them to dinner. It's quite typical and very nicely done.

FLAVIA INVITES JONATHAN, LUPUS ET AL.

Come to a dinner party on the Kalends of December!

There will be warm leeks in garum for a starter

Plus peppered tuna fish garnished with sliced eggs

Then sausage – hot and spicy – for prima mensa,

Together with white beans and red bacon in sauce.

Honey-soaked raisins and roasted chestnuts will finish our fare.

There will be warm, spiced wine to drink throughout,

And for entertainment the trill of a flute and strum of a lyre

Come at the ninth hour and prepare to enjoy yourselves:

You need bring nothing but a clean napkin and polished spoon,

And you won't even need a bodyguard to guide you home!

RECIPES

Here are some recipes for a dinner party, starting with a tasty gustatio, moving on to a prima mensa and finishing with a nice secunda mensa.

PRIMA MENSA – HARE IN A SWEET SAUCE

(Rumour says that eating hare makes you beautiful. This main dish would please any dinner party with female guests.)

Take the hare. Discard the head, feet and entrails. (The dogs will enjoy those.) Skin the hare and chop it into bite sized portions. In an iron saucepan, fry a big onion in olive oil with plenty of garlic and sweet pepper. Add some water, salt, garum and fig syrup about three fingers deep. Cook the pieces of hare in this liquid, adding chopped fennel, carrot and apple. When the pieces of meat, vegetables and fruit are cooked and

tender, put them aside in a ceramic serving bowl kept warm in the hearth below the coals. Continue to cook the liquid on the coals until it becomes thick, like a sauce. Pour this sauce over the pieces of hare and garnish with pinenuts and raisins.

GUSTATIO – ROAST FIG-PECKERS

(fig-peckers are little birds that like to eat figs, hence the name. Jonathan often catches these on sticks smeared with birdlime)

Pluck the little birds dry – without washing them – then skewer them whole on a metal kebab alternating them with plump white mushrooms. Each skewer should have four mushrooms and three little birds. Baste them with honey, sprinkle them with pepper, then grill them well. Serve a skewer to each person.

SECUNDA MENSA – ALMA'S PEAR PATINA

(A patina is a low round straight-sided bowl – usually ceramic – for cooking egg-based dishes)

Take three ripe pears. Peel, core and mash them. Mix in a spoonful of ground cumin and a pinch of pepper. Add four spoonfuls of honey and four of raisin juice. Add some garum, too. This gives it wonderful depth. Finally, beat in six fresh eggs and pour the mixture into a patina. Cook in a medium hot hearth for half an hour. Take out of hearth and let cool. Then slice into wedges.

ALMA'S TOP FIVE MENSAE SECUNDAE (DESSERTS)

1. Slices of watermelon (for a summer dinner party)
2. Grapes and cheese (for an autumn dinner party)
3. A warm egg-custard patina sprinkled with dried mulberries (for winter)
4. Honey pastries in shapes suitable for the celebration
5. Dates stuffed with almonds (simple but delicious)

A ROMAN TIMELINE
BY FLAVIA

Aristo always says that Rome's history is often divided into three sections: the Monarchy, the Republic, and the Empire. The Monarchy begins with the founding of the city by Romulus and lasts through the reigns of the Seven Kings of Rome. The Republic begins with the expulsion of the seventh king and the founding of the Republic, where Rome is ruled by aristocrats. The Empire begins when Octavian takes the title Augustus and becomes the first emperor of Rome.

THE MONARCHY

753 BC   Traditional date for the founding of Rome, Romulus is the first king

715 BC   Numa Pompilius (a Sabine) becomes King 2

673 BC   Tullus Hostilius (a Latin) becomes King 3

641 BC   Ancus Marcius (a Sabine) becomes King 4

616 BC   Tarquinius Priscus (an Etruscan) becomes King 5

579 BC   Servius Tullius (a Latin) becomes King 6

534 BC   Tarquinius Superbus (an Etruscan) becomes King 7

509 BC   Expulsion of Tarquinius Superbus; Roman Republic founded

THE REPUBLIC

508 BC   A brave Roman called Horatius single-handedly holds off Etruscan attackers

378 BC   The Servian wall is built around Rome

323 BC   Death of Alexander the Great

264 BC   First Punic war (against the Phoenicians of Carthage)

241 BC   End of first Punic war

218 BC   Second Punic war (with Hannibal leading Phoenicians)

216 BC   Terrible defeat of Romans at Cannae; 50,000 Romans die

201 BC   End of second Punic war

149 BC   Third Punic war begins

146 BC	Carthage is destroyed by Romans, also Corinth in Greece
73 BC	Slave revolt led by Spartacus begins, lasts three years
70 BC	Cicero's first important speech (according to Aristo)
58 BC	Julius Caesar goes off to conquer Gaul
49 BC	Caesar crosses Rubicon, thereby declaring his intention of taking power
44 BC	Caesar is assassinated
43 BC	Cicero killed by order of Marcus Antonius; head and hands chopped off!
31 BC	Octavian defeats Antonius and Cleopatra at Battle of Actium
30 BC	Suicide of Antonius and Cleopatra

THE EMPIRE

27 BC	Octavian begins to rule as 'Augustus'
3 BC	Jonathan's Messiah, Jesus, born in Judaea
14 AD	Death of Augustus, Tiberius becomes emperor
30 AD	Crucifixion of Jesus in Judaea
37 AD	Caligula becomes emperor, Doctor Mordecai born
41 AD	Claudius becomes emperor
48 AD	Pater and Uncle Gaius are born
50 AD	Jonathan's mother Susannah born
54 AD	Nero becomes emperor
58 AD	My tutor Aristo is born in Corinth
59 AD	Nero has his mother Agrippina murdered
62 AD	Pompeii hit by a bad earthquake (according to pater!)
64 AD	The great fire of Rome, persecution of Jews and Christians under Nero
65 AD	Seneca, Lucan *et al.* commit suicide after their alleged plot against Nero exposed
66 AD	The great Jewish revolt begins in Judaea
68 AD	Nero commits suicide; Nubia, Jonathan and Pulchra born
69 AD	So-called year of the four emperors: Galba, Otho, Vitellius, Vespasian. *I Flavia am born!*

70 AD	Destruction of Jerusalem under command of Titus
71 AD	Lupus born on the island of Symi
73 AD	Destruction of the Jewish stronghold of Masada
79 AD JUNE	Death of Vespasian, Titus becomes emperor
79 AD AUGUST	Eruption of Vesuvius, death of Admiral Pliny
80 AD	Plague and fire in Rome

Note from Caroline Lawrence:
Flavia doesn't know what's coming up in the next year and a half, but *I* do! Here are some of the adventures in store for Flavia and her friends:

80 AD MARCH	The opening of the Colosseum with three months of bloody games
80 AD APRIL	A sea-voyage to Rhodes to find a criminal mastermind
80 AD MAY	A chase across mainland Greece to find the man who stabbed Flavia's father
80 AD JUNE	A visit to the opulent seaside villa where Pulchra lives, to stop a murder
80 AD OCT	A visit to the Circus Maximus to find a missing racehorse
80 AD DEC	A triple murder court case in Ostia and a tragic death
81 AD MARCH	A quest across North Africa for a valuable gemstone
80 AD MAY	A trip down the Nile for Nubia
80 AD JULY	Confronting criminal mastermind in Halicarnassus and Ephesus
81 AD SEPT	Solving the case of the mysterious death of Titus

MAP OF THE ROMAN EMPIRE

DACIA

ESIA
PERIOR

MOESLA IMPERIOR

THRACIA

NIA

EPIRUS

ASIA

BITHNIA ED PONTUS

GALATIA

CAPPADOCIA

ARMENIA

ACHAEA

CILICIA

ASSYRIA

CRETA

LYCIA ET
PAMPHYLIA

CYPRUS

SYRIA

MESOPOTAMIA

JUDAEA

RENAICA

EGYPT

ARABIA
PETRAEA

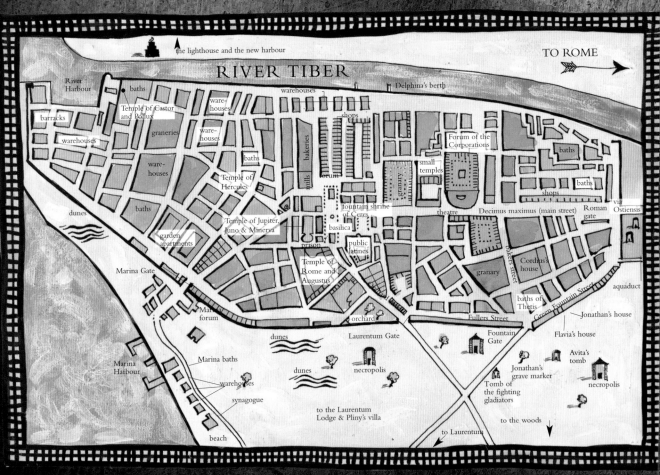

the lighthouse and the new harbour

TO ROME

RIVER TIBER

River Harbour

baths

Delphina's berth

barracks

Temple of Castor and Pollux

ware-houses

warehouses

shops

warehouses

granaries

ware-houses

Forum of the Corporations

baths

baths

ware-houses

baths

small temples

shops

Temple of Hercules

mills

bakeries

granary

theatre

Decimus maximus (main street)

Roman gate

via Ostiensis

dunes

forum

fountain shrine of Ceres

baths

garden apartments

Temple of Jupiter, Juno & Minerva

basilica

prison

public latrines

bakers street

Corditus's house

Marina Gate

Temple of Rome and Augustus

granary

baths of Thetis

Green Fountain Street

aqueduct

Market forum

orchard

Fullers Street

Jonathan's house

Marina baths

dunes

Laurentum Gate

Fountain Gate

Flavia's house

Avita's tomb

Marina Harbour

warehouses

dunes

necropolis

Jonathan's grave marker

necropolis

synagogue

Tomb of the fighting gladiators

to the Laurentum Lodge & Pliny's villa

to the woods

beach

to Laurentum

stables

Shrine of Venus

secret cove

library

entrance to
secret cove

grape
arbour

herb garden

baths

terrace

Polla's suite
(upper colonnade)

guest rooms
(lower colonnade)

docking

VIEW OF THE VILLA OF POLLIUS FELIX IN AD 80

ARISTO'S SCROLL

Achilles (uh-*kill*-eeze)

mythological Greek hero of the Trojan war

Aeneid (uh-*nee*-id)

Virgil's epic poem about Aeneas, the hero whose descendants founded Rome

Alexandria (al-ex-*and*-ree-uh)

capital city of the province of Egypt

amphitheatre (*am*-fee-theatre)

oval-shaped stadium for watching gladiator shows

amphora (*am*-for-uh)

large clay storage jar for holding wine, oil or grain

Antonius (see Marcus Antonius)

Apollodorus (uh-pol-uh-*dor*-uss)

Greek author who wrote an account of the Greek myths

Arion (*air*-ee-on)

mythological king who rode on the back of a dolphin

Asclepiades (uh-skleep-ee-*ah*-deez)

Greek doctor of the 2nd century BC who practised in Rome

atrium (*eh*-tree-um)

reception room in larger Roman homes

Augustus (awe-*guss*-tuss)

first emperor of Rome, ruled from 27BC

Babylon (*bab*-ill-on)

city in Mesopotamia (modern Iraq) with a thriving Jewish community in the 1st century AD

Berenice (bare-uh-*neece*)

(c AD 28 – AD ?) beautiful Jewish Queen, Titus's lover

Britannia (bri-*tan*-ya)

Roman name for the region now known as Britain

Britannicus (bri-*tan*-ick-uss)

son and heir of the Emperor Claudius, possibly poisoned by Nero

caldarium (call-*dar*-ee-um)

hot room in a Roman baths complex

Caligula (ka-*lig*-yoo-la)

third emperor ruled from AD 37-41

Campania (kam-*pane*-yuh)

region around the Bay of Naples

capsa (*kap*-sa)

cylindrical leather case

carruca (ka-*roo*-kuh)

four-wheeled travelling carriage

Carthage (*kar*-thage)

Phoenician city which later became a Roman seaport

Castor (*kas*-tor)

one of the famous twins of Greek mythology

Cato (*kate*-oh)

Marcus Porcius Cato (234-149 BC) wrote a book on agriculture

Ceres (*seer*-eez)

goddess of agriculture and especially grain

Chios (*key*-oss)

Greek island in the Aegean; famous for mastic gum

Cicero (*sis*-sir-ro)

(106-43 BC) famous Roman orator and politician

Circus Maximus (*sir*-kuss *max*-im-uss)

famous racecourse for chariots in Rome

Claudius (*klaw*-dee-uss)

fourth emperor of Rome

Cleopatra (klee-oh-*pat*-ra)

(69–30 BC) Greek ruler of Egypt during the first century BC

Clytemnestra (kly-tem-*nest*-rah)

mythical sister of Helen of Troy and also of Castor and Pollux

Columella (kol-oo-*mel*-uh)

he wrote a book on agriculture

Corinth (*kor*-inth)

important city in the Roman province of Achaea (Greece)

Dies nefasti (*dee*-aze-ne-*fast*-ee)

days in which no legal business could be transacted

Domitian (duh-*mish*-un)

eleventh emporer of Rome, ruled from AD 31–96

Eurydice (your-*id*-iss-ee)

mythological wife of Orpheus

fasti (*fas*-tee)

a calendar marking holidays and business days

forum (*for*-um)

ancient market place and civic centre in a Roman town

freedman (or freedwoman)

a slave who has been set free

garum (*gar*-um)

popular sauce made of fermented fish entrails

Gemini (*jem*-in-eye)

Latin for 'twins'; usually the mythical twins Castor and Pollux

gustatio (guss-*tat*-yo)

first course or 'starter' of a Roman banquet

Herculaneum (herk-you-*lane*-ee-um)

town buried by mud during the eruption of Vesuvius

Hippocrates (hip-pock-rat-eez)

famous Greek doctor who lived in the 5th century BC

Hispania (hiss-*pan*-ya)

Roman for the region now known as Spain

Horace (*hore*-uss)

(65 – 8 BC) famous Latin poet

Ides (eyedz)

15th day of March, May, July, October

Isis (*eye*-siss)

Egyptian goddess

Jerusalem (j'-*roo*-sah-lem)

capital of the Roman province of Judaea, destroyed in AD 70

Judaea (joo-*dee*-uh)

Roman name for the area now known as Israel

Juvenal (*joo*-ven-al)

(c. AD 60 – c. 135) witty Roman poet

Kalends (kal-ends)

1st day of Roman month

lararium (lar-*ar*-ee-um)

household shrine

Laurentum (lore-*ent*-um)

village on the coast of Italy a few miles south of Ostia

Leptis Magna (*lep*-tiss *mag*-nuh)

Roman town in North Africa

Livia (*liv*-ee-uh)

wife of Rome's first emperor, Augustus

Livy (*liv*-ee)

(c. 59 BC – c. AD 17) famous Roman historian

Ludi Romani (*loo*-dee ro-*mah*-nee)

games (especially chariot races) in honour of Jupiter

Lucan (*loo*-kan)

Roman poet who was forced to commit suicide by Nero

lustratio (luss-*tra*-tee-oh)

purification ceremony usually involving the sacrifice of an animal

Maecenas (my-*see*-nass)

(70 – 8 BC) patron to poets

Marcus Antonius (*mar*-kuss an-*tone*-ee-uss)

(83 – 30 BC) AKA Mark Anthony, statesman and soldier

Martial (*marsh*-all)

(40 AD – c. 104) witty Roman poet

Masada (m'-*sah*-duh)

famous Jewish stronghold in the Judaean desert near the Dead Sea

Massilia (muh-*sill*-ya)

Roman seaport (modern Marseilles)

Mithras (*mith*-rass)

Persian god whose cult spread throughout the Roman world

Mouseion (moo-*zay*-on)

famous centre of learning in Alexandria

murmillo (mur-*mill*-oh)

heavily armed gladiator, often had a fish design on his helmet

Neapolis (nee-*ap*-o-liss)

a large city in the south of Italy near Vesuvius; modern Naples

necropolis (ne-*krop*-oh-liss)

graveyard of a Roman town

Nero (*near*-oh)

fifth Emperor of Rome from AD 54 – 68

Nones (nonz)

7th day of March, May, July, October; 5th day

of the others

Octavian (ok-*tave*-ee-un)

earlier name of Rome's first Emperor: Augustus

Orpheus (*or*-fee-uss)

skilled musician in Greek mythology

Ostia (*oss*-tee-uh)

port of ancient Rome

palaestra (puh-*lice*-tra)

exercise area of public baths

palla (*pal*-uh)

a woman's cloak

pantomime (*pan*-toe-mime)

story told through dance and music

Parentalia (pare-en-*tall*-ya)

Roman festival of the dead

pater (*pa*-tare)

Latin for 'father'

paterfamilias (*pa*-tare fa-*mill*-ee-us)

father and protector of the household

patina (puh-*teen*-uh)

Latin for 'dish' or 'pan': a kind of flan

patrician (puh-*trish*-un)

highest Roman class

patron (*pay*-tron)

someone who has 'clients' dependent on him

Plautus (*plow*-tuss)

(c. 254 – c.184 BC) Roman playwright

Pliny (*plin*-ee) the Elder

(c AD 23 – 79) scholar who died in eruption of Vesuvius

Pliny (plin-ee) the Younger

(c AD 61 – 111) nephew of Pliny the Elder

poculum (*pock*-yoo-lum)

a cup; sometimes referring to the drink inside

Pollux (*pol*-luks)

one of the famous twins of Greek mythology

Pompeii (pom-*pay*)

Roman town destroyed by Vesuvius in AD 79

Portus (*por*-tuss)

man-made harbour a few miles north of Ostia

posca (*poss*-kuh)

well-watered vinegar

prima mensa (*pree*-ma *men*-sa)

main course of a meal

Puteoli (poo-tee-*oh*-lee)

port on the bay of Naples

quadriga (*kwad*-rig-uh)

a chariot pulled by four horses

retiarius (ret-ee-*are*-ee-uss)

gladiator who fought with net, trident and dagger

Romulus (*rom*-yoo-luss)

mythical founder of Rome

salutatio (sal-oo-*tah*-tee-oh)

formal morning visit of a client to patron

Saturnalia (sat-ur-*nail*-yuh)

festival of Saturn, celebrating the mid-winter solstice

secunda mensa (sek-*oon*-da *men*-sa)

dessert or last course of a meal

secutor (*seck*-you-tor)

gladiator with a smooth tight helmet

Seneca (*sen*-eh-kuh)

(c. BC 4 – AD 65) Stoic philosopher and tutor to Nero

sesterces (sess-*tur*-seez)

plural of 'sestercius', a brass coin

sportula (*sport*-yoo-lah)

gift of food or money from patron to client

Stabia (*stah*-byah)

town south of Pompeii

stola (*stole*-uh)

a long tunic worn by women

strigil (*strij*-ill)

curved bronze tool for scraping off at the baths

stylus (*stile*-us)

tool for writing on wax tablets

succah (*sook*-uh)

a shelter woven of branches for the Jewish Feast of Tabernacles

sudatorium (soo-da-*tor*-ee-um)

room of the baths designed to make people sweat

Surrentum (sir-*wren*-tum)

modern Sorrento, south of Naples

tesserae (*tess*-ur-eye)

the tiny chips that make up the picture in a mosaic

Titus (*tie*-tuss)

tenth emperor of Rome, ruled from AD 79 – 81

toga virilis (*toe*-ga vir-*ill*-iss)

toga a boy put on when he came of age

Torah (*tor*-uh)

word for Hebrew Bible

triclinium (trik-*lin*-ee-um)

ancient Roman dining room, with three couches

verna (*vur*-nuh)

person born into slavery

Vespasian (vess-*pay*-zhun)

ninth emporer of Rome, ruled from AD 69 – 79

Vesuvius (vuh-*soov*-yuss)

famous volcano, which erupted on 24 August AD 79

Via Ostiensis (*vee*-uh os-tee-*en*-suss)

the road connecting Rome and Ostia

vigiles (*vij*-il-lays)

watchmen who guarded the town against robbery and fire

Virgil (*vur*-jill)

Publius Vergilius Maro (7 – 19 BC) famous Latin poet

Vulcanalia (vul-kan-*ale*-ya)

festival of the blacksmith god Vulcan

THE LAST SCROLL
BY CAROLINE LAWRENCE

Like Flavia, I would love my books to be read two thousand years from now. But I'm quite content that many children are reading them today, and learning about some of my favourite characters from the past. If you read my Roman Mysteries series, you will meet brave Pliny the Elder, the somewhat nerdish Pliny the Younger, the enigmatic Titus and the despicable but fascinating Nero.

There is also the poet Martial, whom I love and hate with equal enthusiasm. I love him because he writes about the minutiae of ancient Rome, things like socks made of goats' hair, a back-scratcher in the shape of a hand, a double-sided gaming board given as a Saturnalia present. He describes people in a vivid, humorous way: the elderly man who thinks people will be fooled by combing a few strands of hair over his bald pate, the dinner-party guest who pretends to pick his teeth with an ivory toothpick but has no teeth, the youth who fancies himself a ladies' man even though he has the face of 'a man swimming underwater'. But I also hate Martial because he loved to make obscene and sometimes cruel jokes at other people's expense. He would have been about forty years old when my books take place. He makes a brief appearance in *The Gladiators from Capua:*

On Julia's other side sat an ape-like man with hairy arms and legs, and eyebrows that met over his nose. He was taking notes on a wax tablet . . .

'Where once was water now is dry land,' Nubia heard the hairy-armed man proclaim.

'Virgil?' asked Domitian.

'My own verse,' said the poet, looking smug. 'I have just composed it.'

The Gladiators from Capua, pp 124–125

Sometimes, while writing the Roman Mysteries, I feel like a detective myself. I have made some exciting discoveries about the ancient world.

For example, while researching *The Enemies of Jupiter* I watched a documentary on TV claiming that angry Jews might have started the 'Great Fire' of Nero's reign. The arguments proposed by the scholars did not convince me, because AD 64 was before the Jewish revolt, before the destruction of Jerusalem, before the mass suicide of Masada. It occurred to me that if any fire had been set by Jewish zealots, it would have been the later, less famous fire which devastated Rome in AD 80, sixteen years after Nero's 'Great Fire'. Here are the arguments:

- By AD 80, the Jews had rebelled against Rome and lost everything in the gamble.
- Titus — the commander who had subdued Judaea, taken Jerusalem and destroyed the Temple of God — had just become emperor. After the destruction of Jerusalem, the rabbis had predicted that God's wrath would fall upon Rome if the hated Titus ever came to power.
- The fire of AD 80 probably started at the Temple of Jupiter, the symbol *par excellence* of Rome.
- This temple was maintained by taxes formerly paid by Jews for the maintenance of their own Temple, now destroyed.
- The fire of AD 80 occurred during the Jewish festival of Purim, when Jews commemorate victory over their persecutors.
- The fire of AD 80 occurred 666 years after the destruction of the First Temple by the Babylonians in 586 BC. 666 is the Biblical number of the Beast. Many scholars think the Beast is Nero, because the Hebrew letters of 'Nero Caesar' add up to 666. Nero

blamed the fire of AD 64 on Jews as well as Christians, and killed many of them in terrible ways.

- The fire of AD 80 took place only a month or two before the opening of the Colosseum, a 'pagan' monument built with spoils from Jerusalem and by Jewish slave labour. It was expected that many more Jews would be killed for amusement during the games themselves.

- The fire of AD 80 was a terrible fire, and – like 'Nero's fire' – it burned for three days. It would have devastated central Rome if the wind direction had been different.

As far as I know, no one else has suggested this possibility: that Jews started the fire of AD 80. So I thought I would play with the idea in *The Enemies of Jupiter*.

After writing the first draft of book eight in the series, *The Gladiators from Capua*, I sent a few passages to the world-expert on the Flavian Amphi-

Caroline and Simon Callow (who plays Pliny) laughing together on the set of Roman Mysteriews.

theatre (Colosseum) in the time of Titus: Professor Kathleen Colman at Harvard. Although she was busy teaching, administrating and doing research, she told me she would read the entire manuscript. She did this, and one evening she phoned me from Harvard and took me through the whole book, helping me get the details exactly right. After the book was published we met for the first time in London, and she told me she had been one of the historical advisors for the film *Gladiator*. They didn't use many of her suggestions, so it was gratifying for her when I took the advice she gave me.

Another thing I did while researching *The Gladiators from Capua* was to attend a bullfight in Spain. Bullfights are the closest modern spectacle to the beast fights held in Roman arenas. There are an astounding number of similarities. The main thing that struck me is that only if you had one of the best seats near the front would you have been able to see the blood spurt and smell the fear and hear the animals grunt in pain. The higher you go in the arena, the more unreal the whole spectacle becomes. I realised that watching a spectacle from the highest level of the Colosseum – where women and children sat – would have been the equivalent of watching a big-budget action film on a tiny iPod screen.

Another way I do research is by reading dozens and dozens of books. My flat in London is full of books. They cover the walls, are piled on the floor and tables, even spill into the bathroom. For *The Sirens of Surrentum* I had to read lots of books about poisons. For *The Charioteer of Delphi* I read a fascinating book by an autistic woman called Temple Grandin who has a special rapport with animals. She was partly the inspiration for Scopas, the charioteer from Delphi.

I visit all the places my books are set. This has meant trips to the Greek Islands for *The Colossus of Rhodes*; to Athens, Delphi and Corinth for *The Fugitive from Corinth*; to the Bay of Naples for *The Sirens of Surrentum*; to Morocco and Libya for *The Beggar of Volubilis* and to Egypt for *The Scribes from Alexandria*. I want to see what flowers would have been in bloom, what food would have been in season, which birds would have been in the trees.

I've seen Sciron's Rock on the Saronic Gulf near Corinth, and heard about bubbling sulphur water and blood-red rain from my friends who live in Ostia. I have been to Rhodes and seen that there is not a scrap left of the great Colossus. I have been to the beautiful island of Symi, Lupus's birthplace, and seen the sponges they used to bring up. I found mastic gum in a little shop on the island of Cos.

I have had some magical experiences, like watching the sun set on the longest day of the year from the ruins of the villa of Pollius Felix. Or finding a natural spring of water at Cenchrea, one of Corinth's ancient ports. On the island of Ischia in the Bay of Naples, I had a 'bath' in black mud, like the one Lupus experiences in *The Sirens of Surrentum*. In Fez, Morocco, I went to a hammam (a public bath-house) which had different hours for men and women, a central changing room, a warm room with stone basins of hot and cold water – and buckets to mix them, plus a steam room with underfloor fires to heat it: just like the ancient Roman baths.

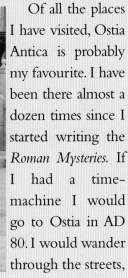

Of all the places I have visited, Ostia Antica is probably my favourite. I have been there almost a dozen times since I started writing the *Roman Mysteries*. If I had a timemachine I would go to Ostia in AD 80. I would wander through the streets, visit the baths, shop in the forum and watch the ships disgorge their exotic cargoes and passengers. Then I would take a mule-cart up to Rome. Sadly, nobody has yet invented a timemachine, but I hope this book and the others in my series will help transport you to that ancient and fascinating world.

ACKNOWLEDGEMENTS

All photographs, excluding those on pages 67, 88 and 119, supplied courtesy of The Little Entertainment Group.

The Little Entertainment Group are proud to bring the Roman world of AD 79 to the small screen. *Roman Mysteries* is a landmark production shot entirely on location in Tunisia and Malta, featuring a cast and crew of 150, making it undoubtedly the UK's biggest children's television drama to date.

Formed in 1988, The Little Entertainment Group is a leading Production, Post Production and Rights Management company. Early high profile audio post projects including *Casper the Friendly Ghost*, *Barney*, *Magic Roundabout* and *Watership Down* led to a full production debut series *Billy* for ITV, which won the Golden Pulcinella award for best new character. Closely followed in 1999 by *Merlin the Magical Puppy*, also for ITV, this stop-frame series was entirely created, designed, animated and post-produced by The Little Entertainment Group. This success led to the production of *Little Red Tractor* — a series that was developed into three commissions from the BBC totalling 75 episodes.

The Little Entertainment Group is exclusively focused on producing and exploiting high-end Children's and Family entertainment and we are passionately committed to becoming the leading Production and Rights management operation within this genre.

For more information, please visit our website:
http://www.thelittleentertainmentgroup.co.uk

THE ROMAN MYSTERIES

Also available: